THE SECRET SERVICE

The CIA want retired Secret Service agent Jackson back on a mission: to foil Operation Condor, a top secret plan conceived by the East German security police in the Cold War, and now in the hands of *al-Qaeda*. But he finds that he is being used as the bait in a trap. His only chance of escape is to discover who passed the plan to *al-Qaeda*. And he suspects that the answer lies in the Caribbean island of Barbados.

RAFE McGREGOR

THE
SECRET
SERVICE

Complete and Unabridged

LINFORD
Leicester

First published in Great Britain

First Linford Edition
published 2008

British Library CIP Data

McGregor, Rafe
  The Secret Service.—Large print ed.—
Linford mystery library
  1. Suspense fiction
  2. Large type books
  I. Title
  823.9′2 [F]

ISBN 978–1–84782–221–5

Published by
F. A. Thorpe (Publishing)
Anstey, Leicestershire

Set by Words & Graphics Ltd.
Anstey, Leicestershire
Printed and bound in Great Britain by
T. J. International Ltd., Padstow, Cornwall

This book is printed on acid-free paper

To Christine Naylor:
For
All the help and support:
past, present, and future.

Prologue

Anti-Terror Colonel Killed in Contact

Colonel Gary Brukman, 34, of the US Marine Corps, was killed in an attack by insurgents in northern Iraq yesterday.

Colonel Brukman, the commanding officer of the 4th Marine Expeditionary Brigade (Anti-Terrorism), was a prominent figure in the War on Terror.

He was on a routine patrol with a unit from his Brigade outside Haditha, near the Syrian border, when his command came under fire.

A second soldier, Sergeant Johann Hausser, 40, was also killed in the ambush.

Colonel Brukman, from Baltimore, joined the Marine Corps in 1989. He served in Desert Shield and Desert Storm, and with the 2nd Recon Battalion at Camp Lejeune, before joining the Anti-Terrorism Brigade as a major in

2001. He served with the Brigade in Operation Enduring Freedom in Afghanistan and Djibouti, and was promoted to lieutenant-colonel at the beginning of the Second Gulf War.

His leadership and devotion to duty have been recognised by numerous decorations and by his unprecedented promotion to commanding officer earlier this year, which made him the youngest full colonel in the US Armed Forces.

A DoD spokesperson called Colonel Brukman an 'American hero' and a 'true patriot'. The Colonel is survived by his wife, both parents, and two younger brothers, one of whom is serving in Iraq as an officer in the Army.

USA Today, 12 September 2006

1

The Staatssicherheitsdienst

It was exactly twenty-past eight on Monday morning when Detective Inspector Moon and Detective Sergeant Sommer watched the tall, blonde woman walk out of 39 Birch Tree Grove. She pressed the remote on her key fob and climbed into the blue Tigra convertible parked in the driveway.

'Now that's one hell of a good-looking lady,' said the Middle-Eastern man in the back of the unmarked Astra. His voice was very deep, and his accent rich New York.

'Reminds me of Elle Macpherson,' said Sommer.

She reversed the Tigra out the drive way, and then pulled off, passing the policemen without a glance. Moon looked at Sommer, then Hassoun, and nodded. They all climbed out of the car and crossed the road to number thirty-nine. Moon glanced at his colleagues one more time before knocking loudly on the front door.

The man who opened it was wearing a dark blue dressing gown, with bare feet. He was shorter than Moon, stocky, with short brown hair streaked with premature grey, and a long, ugly scar running down his left cheek. When he spoke his voice was deadpan, as emotionless as the lack of expression on his face: 'Dave.'

'Jackson.'

Jackson stood motionless in the door-way, his face as emotionless as his voice.

'Well, are you going to let us freeze to death out here, or what?' said Moon.

Jackson turned and walked off. Moon led Sommer and Hassoun into the lounge, where Jackson was already seated on a comfortable leather chair. The three men sat on the matching sofa opposite him.

'I'd hoped never to see either of you again. And nothing on earth could make me work for SO12, no matter what you threaten me with this time.' His accent was difficult to place, somewhere between Irish and Dutch, perhaps.

Moon was unperturbed. 'We haven't come to enlist your services, we've come to introduce you to Mr Hassoun. Mr Hassoun is from the Company, and he has some information he'd like to share with you.'

'One of the perks of not working in the intelligence community anymore is that I don't have to put up with all the jargon and doublespeak. So you can tell me exactly *who* and *what* Hassoun is before we continue.'

Anger flashed across Moon's face, but Hassoun stood up, stepped towards Jackson, and offered his hand, 'Erik Hassoun. It's a pleasure to meet you, Mr Jackson. I'm with the Central Intelligence Agency.' Jackson stared at Hassoun and his outstretched hand. 'And the inspector's quite right, he's only here to facilitate our meeting. I've been looking for you for some time, and I thought it might be better if I had a proper introduction.'

'Looking for me?'

Hassoun sat back down. 'Yeah, not for you in particular, you understand, but for a man to do a job for me.'

Jackson held up his hand, 'No way, Mr Hassoun. You heard what I said. I've got two jobs now: one in an outdoor shop on the high street, the other with mountain rescue — more like *hill* rescue here, actually. I don't make much money, but they're both nice and easy — just the way I like it — and more than enough to keep me busy. So I'm sorry if Dave and John have wasted your time, but I'd like you all to leave now.' He rose.

Hassoun's next words were quick, staccato: 'What if I told you your brother-in-law was murdered by the Stasi?'

Jackson, still standing, smiled. 'I'd say you've got the wrong brother-in-law: mine died in combat in Iraq last year.'

'Colonel Brukman didn't die in combat. He was shot by one of his men, Sergeant Hausser, a Stasi-trained assassin.'

Jackson hesitated. 'The Stasi? I was under the impression that *Stasi* was short for *Staatssicherheitsdienst*, the former

East German State Security Police.'

'You betcha.'

Jackson put his hands in the pockets of his robe. 'Everyone who watched the Wall come down knows that the Stasi were disbanded, so how the fuck can they be murdering people twenty-five years later?'

'If you'll allow me a minute, Mr Jackson, I'll tell you exactly how.'

Jackson sat back down.

'In 1988 a Stasi brigadier in their foreign section named Paul Berger launched Operation Condor. Six sleepers were sent to the West, under the pretence of having fled the Eastern Bloc to start new lives in the US and Europe. None of them had any previous connection with the Stasi, and none claimed to have any useful information for our intelligence services. There was absolutely nothing to distinguish them from the thousands before and after them who escaped the Iron Curtain.'

'Sleepers? You mean agents that lead normal lives until they're activated by their handlers?'

'Yeah, that's right. It was a big thing in

the Cold War, getting popular again now too. Berger reported directly to Mielke, the head of the Stasi, and the sleepers were trained by the KGB for extra security. And it *was* extra secure, because the KGB didn't even know what they were training the guys for. Only four men knew about Operation Condor . . . '

'I don't doubt there were — and probably are — Eastern Bloc sleepers out there . . . out here even. But there's no East and West anymore, so what does it matter? These sleepers of yours will sleep the rest of their lives and no one'll ever know any better.'

'Not these ones,' Hassoun shook his head. 'Operation Condor wasn't a home team for the Stasi. It was set in motion to assist Middle-Eastern terrorists, we think the PLO. Berger thought it would be useful to the Arabs to have assassins that were European, as opposed to Middle-Eastern. It's quite a good idea, don't you think? I mean if you and me are walkin' down the street and they've got the cops looking for a Moslem terrorist, which one of us are they gonna stop and search?' Hassoun grinned, showing straight, white teeth, 'It ain't gonna be you, is it?'

Jackson waited a while before answering. 'Everyone knows that East Germans were sponsoring Arab terrorists back in the eighties, but why would the PLO want to kill my brother-in-law?'

'Operation Condor never reached the people it was intended for. The records were destroyed and it stayed with Berger, who fled — to South America, we think — in 1990. We're of the opinion that the operation is now in the hands of *al-Qaeda*.'

'*Al-Qaeda*! Gary was killed on September 11 last year . . . but no, why would a Stasi brigadier sell the sleepers to *al-Qaeda*?'

'Money, bitterness against the West? I couldn't tell you. But your brother-in-law was killed by one of his sergeants, Johann Hausser. On the same day, a security guard attempted to kill President Bush in an underground parking lot in Phoenix, and Major-General Matheson, the US Task Force Commander in Kabul, was wounded by a policeman from Pittsburgh. You won't find anything about the President in the papers, but you can check on the other two. You'll find that Sergeant Hausser was born in Dresden, and that General Matheson was wounded by shrapnel from a grenade thrown by an American cop — also on September 11. Dietrich, the cop, was from Pittsburgh and had flown out to Afghanistan a few days before. You wanna hazard a guess as to where he was born?'

'The German Democratic Republic?'

'You catch on fast, Mr Jackson. He was born in Templin, in East Germany.'

'This is unbelievable.'

'Don't you kid me! What's more believable, the Stasi slipping some sleepers to their allies before they bow out, or a buncha rag-heads killing three thousand people by flying jumbo jets into the Twin Towers. What do you think?'

'You said there were six sleepers.'

'Yeah. Three were sent into the US, two to England, and one to France.'

'What about the other three?'

'Nothing, yet. *Al-Qaeda* are probably

waiting to coordinate them with other attacks. But we know who they are, all three of them.'

'You know?'

'We sure do.'

'I thought you said only four people knew about Operation Condor? One was Mielke. He died in 2000. You don't know where Berger is, so your informant must be one of the other two. Who is it?'

'Colonel Kurt Schellong was the only other Stasi agent who knew about Operation Condor. He and his family were killed in a car crash near their home in Spain in 1998. The fourth guy was Lieutenant Colonel Vladimir Kaminski of the KGB. He was one of the guys the Russians sent over to East Germany at the end of 1989 to gather up any embarrassing files the Stasi might have lying around. He retired just before Mielke died.'

'He told you?'

'We never got the chance to ask: he disappeared at the end of 2000. No one's seen him since.'

'So, if there's a plan so secret that only

four people in the Eastern Bloc intelligence community know about it, and all four are now dead or missing, how the hell did *you* find out about it? You don't expect me to believe that the Stasi or *al-Qaeda* were so amateur as to let the sleepers know one another's identities, do you?'

'No, of course not. Anyway, we didn't get the opportunity to interrogate any of the assassins, they were all shot dead. We got the information about Operation Condor from a Stasi memo.'

Jackson laughed, and the scar on the side of his face crinkled. Hassoun wasn't quite sure if he was smiling or not. 'You really must think I was born yesterday, Hassoun. The Stasi, as one would expect for an organisation of that nature, destroyed any and all incriminating documents. I read about the lengths they went to, to get rid of all the shit they had. And now you're telling me that this, perhaps their highest classified operation, was just left lying around somewhere? To turn up with the CIA twenty-five years later? I really think it's time you all left,' he stood up again.

'You must be out of touch, Mr Jackson, if you don't know the answer to your own question. It's no secret that for the past eleven years we've been reassembling Stasi files.'

'Reassembling?'

'That's right. A great deal of the Stasi paperwork was just shredded and left in bags. We've had the bags for years, but we've only recently acquired a machine that re-assembles shredded material.' Jackson stared at him. 'It's pretty slow, which is why we only found out about Operation Condor after Colonel Brukman was murdered, and why we've only just tracked down the three European sleepers. But it's true. You can check the bit about the reassembling out on the CNN website, or anywhere for that matter.'

Jackson sat down again. 'Okay, what if I do believe you. What you need to do is find whoever Berger handed the operation to, don't you?'

'Exactly right, Mr Jackson. In an ideal world, we'd hunt down Berger, and he'd lead us to whoever's running Operation Condor now. But that ain't gonna happen. We've been trying to find Berger since he disappeared in 1990. Even if he is alive, there's no way we'll find him now. As for Condor's new controller — well, let's just say we haven't had a lotta success breaking into *al-Qaeda* as it is.'

'So what are you going to do? More importantly, why are you here?'

'We're taking the easy option, Mr Jackson. We're gonna kill the three remaining sleepers before anyone activates them. And that's where you come in.'

Jackson stood up again and walked to the door.

'Where are you going?' said Hassoun.

'To make us some coffee.'

2

Condorman

Ten minutes later Hassoun resumed: 'I need a man to kill the three sleepers. When I saw that Colonel Brukman's brother-in-law was a former South African Secret Service agent living in England, well, I thought you might just like to do it for us.'

'You've got agents all over the place, why me?'

'Because the Company doesn't do it's own dirty work, we contract out. You know that. When I found out that you'd already done some work for SO12 — our Special Branch pals in London's finest — since your retirement, I approached Inspector Moon. He tells me that you're more than qualified for the job. So that's why I asked him to introduce us, and that's why I'm sitting here drinkin' your coffee.'

Jackson pointed his finger at Moon, who was toying with his own cup. 'And you think I'll work for you again because it involves my brother-in-law?'

'Something like that, *mate*.'

Jackson turned back to Hassoun, 'You want these men killed?'

'That's exactly what I want, and exactly what I'm gonna get, with or without your help.'

'Who are they?'

'The first lives in Colchester, where he works for a company called Murray Drills and Demolition; the second works on an oil rig off Aberdeen; the third is in Marseilles. So how about some travel on us, Mr Jackson? First-class of course.'

'A demolition company?'

'Yeah, and an engineer on an oil rig. You'll no doubt have noticed that all of the sleepers put themselves in occupations where they would have access to arms and training. The Americans were a soldier, a cop, and a security guard. But cops and security guards aren't armed here, so the British guys went for jobs with explosives. You can see why we want these guys dead.'

'What about me?'

'I'm not with you, Mr Jackson.'

'Murder is a crime in Britain, Mr Hassoun, even CIA-sanctioned murder. I don't want to spend the rest of my life in jail thanks very much.'

'That's not gonna happen. We're gonna set you up with everything you need and arrange everything for you. The inspector and his SO12 guys are gonna make sure they keep an eye on you just in case you need a little help getting away from the cops, not that it'll come to that.'

'It'd better not come to that,' said Moon.

'Are you going to give me another identity again?' Jackson asked him.

'Of course. Three, in fact. Driver's license, credit cards, expense accounts; and a passport for the trip to France.'

'How long are you expecting this to take?'

'A couple of weeks for the whole thing,' said Hassoun. 'We've already got tabs on the sleepers. This is gonna be the easiest assignment you've ever had, Mr Jackson.

But be warned, these guys won't be expecting trouble of any sort. They got wives, kids, families, lives. I don't want you seizing up at the last minute because someone gives his baby daughter a cuddle.'

'If I agree to work for you all three will die, but no one else. Is that clear?'

'That's all I want, just the three of them. Like I said, it's gonna be dead easy.' He smiled, showing another flash of white, 'Just like shootin' fish in a barrel.'

'*If* I agree, when do I start?'

'Tomorrow first thing,' said Moon.

Jackson turned back to Hassoun. 'In that case, there's two things I'm going to need.'

'And what're they?'

'Equipment for the job.'

'Oh, I got plenty of that, don't worry. In fact, I've got Gary Brukman's Colt .45 service pistol for you. I thought there might be some kinda poetic justice in that,' he smiled, 'What else?'

'Permission from my wife.' Jackson stood up.

'I can't help you with that.'

'You already have and you know it.'

'I have?' Hassoun feigned innocence.

'I promised her I wouldn't do any more intelligence work after my job for SO12 two years ago,' he indicated Moon and Sommer.

'You did quite a job, I heard. Killed a buncha terrorists?'

'You know better than to ask me about that, Hassoun, and you also know that doing something to help avenge my wife's little sister might just be the one way she'll let me break my promise. It's time you left now.'

The three men rose.

Moon handed Jackson a small mobile phone. 'Phone me on that as soon as you've made your mind up. I need twelve hours to set everything up, so don't drag your heels.'

Jackson saw them out.

Back in the car, Hassoun was in good spirits. 'I think a celebration will be in order, come lunch-time, gentlemen. We'll stop off at one of those bars, what do you call them over here . . . *pubs*?'

'He hasn't agreed yet,' said Moon, glancing over his shoulder.

'He will.'

'Yeah, he will,' said Sommer.

'Come on, Inspector, don't rain on my parade here.'

'We'll celebrate if and when he calls.'

'Okay, have it your way. You sure he's what we want, our *Condorman*?'

'Condorman?'

'You never saw the movie — with your guy Oliver Reed?'

'No.'

'Well, never mind. Will Jackson take care of Lombard?'

'Yeah.'

'Then there's just one other thing: should we really be giving him the different identities?'

'Yeah.'

'You sure?'

'Yeah.'

Hassoun look unconvinced.

'Everyone recognises him,' said Sommer, 'it's the scar that does it.'

★   ★   ★

At half-past six that evening Jackson rang the pre-programmed number in the mobile phone. There was a recorded message from Sommer:

The Red Lion Hotel, Colchester, Tuesday at one o'clock. At the top of the stairs it's left to reception, straight ahead into The Parliament Restaurant and bar. A man named Parker will be waiting. Big, black geezer. Hassoun's man. Bring an overnight bag only, no ID.

That was all.

3

Snaiperskaya Vintovka Dragunov

Parker was sitting at a corner table in The Parliament Restaurant. He was wearing a smart dark suit and reading *USA Today*. He glanced at his watch: five minutes past one. Still no sign of the South African. Two minutes later he looked up to see a heavily-built man with a long scar on his face and a sports bag over his shoulder enter the bar area. He was wearing a black suede leather jacket and beige chinos. The man walked over to him.

'Jackson.'

'Parker?'

'Charlie Parker — an' before you say it, yeah, just like the musician.'

'What musician?'

Parker scowled, 'Sit down and let's get this over and done with.' He sat and Parker checked the restaurant and the bar. Both empty, no other customers and no staff. 'After we've had this little talk, go to reception and book in as a Mr John Pearl of 16 Sutton Avenue, Horsfield, Bristol. You'll be given room one. Inside you'll find an ice hockey bag hanging up in the wardrobe. In the bag you'll find a field-stripped Dragunov SVD sniper rifle, Colonel Brukman's forty-five, and a Glock G19 — the compact one. There's plenty of ammo for everything, as well as two cleaning kits and a file on Lombard. Also, there's a wallet with money, credit cards and a driver's licence in the names of John Pearl and John Silver. You following?'

'Ja.'

'When you're done, walk down to the NCP car park in Osborne Street. At the north end of the second level you'll find a blue Vauxhall Cavalier. The keys are on top of the rear left wheel. The car is hired out in Pearl's name. Take the car and drive out to a village south of here called Layer del la Haye. You got it?'

'Ja.'

'Find Rectory Hill. On Rectory Hill opposite an old church you'll find the Old

Hall Community. It's a commune. Lombard lives there . . . '

'He lives in a commune?'

'Yeah.'

'You're sure?'

'Of course I'm fucking sure.'

'Don't you find that a little strange, an assassin living in a commune?'

'No, why the hell should I?'

'I thought you said he works for a demolitions company?'

'Yeah, he does.'

'But he lives in a commune?'

'Yeah. Well, he's a *communist*, whadya expect?'

Jackson's scar twitched, but he said nothing.

'Right. The commune has only one entrance and exit. Across the road from that are some houses with good tree cover. There's one called The Limes, as in *limeys*, you got it?'

'*Ja*.'

'You're booked in here for two nights. In the early hours of Thursday morning you'll drive out to Layer de la Haye, park up in the car park of the Red Lion

— that's the bar in the village, I guess they musta ran outta names around here — and cut through the churchyard to access The Limes from the rear. The house will be empty and the key for the back door is in the bag in your room. You'll take up position in one of the upper windows with the Dragunov. Some time between quarter-past seven and quarter-to eight Lombard will come out of the entrance to the commune in a bright blue Smartcar. The gate is on a sharp bend in the road, so he'll have to stop to check left and right. When he does, you whack him. Got it?'

'Ja.'

'Leave the rifle where it is, go back to the car. Drive back to the car park and leave the car as you found it. Come back here, check out, and ditch the Pearl ID. Get on the train for Kings' Cross, London, as Silver. Buy a ticket for Aberdeen. Before you get there I'll be in touch on the cell you've got. Got it?'

'Ja.'

'I'm told you can use a Dragunov. Can you?'

'*Ja.*'

'You don't say much. Any questions?'

'Where can I test the rifle?'

'You wanna test it?'

'*Ja.*'

'Christ, it's accurate to one thousand three hunnerd metres; you're gonna be shootin' this sonofabitch at about twenny. I thought you said you could use it?'

'I can, but I'd still like to test it.'

'Well, you don't get to test it. It's already been sighted by one of our guys. That's why we gave you a semi-auto, in case you miss. You've got ten rounds in the magazine, for Chrissakes.'

'Is Lombard the only one who uses the car?'

'I don't know, but he'll be in it that morning. Anyway, that's what the photos in your file are for. Anything else?'

'You said the forty-five was Brukman's service pistol.'

'Yeah, 1911 model, silver-plated with pearl handle grips, real neat piece of artillery. *Pearl, Silver*, guess what you're third ID is?'

'I thought the American army changed

to a 9mm pistol in the eighties, to fit in with the rest of NATO.'

'They did, but Brukman liked the forty-five. Carried it everywhere with him. What's that gotta do with anything?'

'I like to know what's going on. I find I live longer that way.'

'Wise guy, huh? Don't you trust me, or sometin'?' Parker was becoming irritated, 'By the time you check in, I'll be outta here and you won't be able to get hold of me. So, is that all?'

'*Ja.*' Jackson stood up and picked up his bag.

Parker watched him walk to the door. 'Pearl.'

Jackson turned.

Parker cocked an imaginary gun with his fingers, pointed it at Jackson, and silently pulled the trigger.

★   ★   ★

Moon and Sommer were waiting for Hassoun when he entered The Volunteer in Marylebone at midday on Thursday. Moon assumed he'd chosen the pub because it was close to the US Embassy in Grosvenor Square. He arrived at the table with a round of drinks, a menu, and a cheerful grin, 'Good day, gentleman, an' what a fine day it's turning out to be.'

'Alright,' said Moon taking his pint of Stella.

'Cheers,' said Sommer, lifting his.

'Cheers it is indeed,' said Hassoun, toasting them, 'You've heard the good news, have you?'

Moon took a long draught of the lager and put the glass back on the table. 'Lombard was shot outside his residence at zero-seven-twenty-two this morning. An unidentified sniper used an SDV Dragunov 7.62mm sniper rifle, firing two shots: one in the chest, one in the head. He died immediately. His wife was in the car with him; she was unharmed. The Essex Constabulary have no leads as to the identity of the gunman.'

'I can match that, Inspector, because Jackson got on a train at eight fifty-five this morning. Unfortunately he didn't do quite what we told him. Instead of coming back into London, he headed to Norwich, then picked up the northbound train at Peterborough. Does he often do this?'

'Do what?'

'Not follow instructions.'

'He's switched-on,' said Sommer.

'He killed Lombard, didn't he?' Moon replied.

'Yeah, he did, but I — we — need to know where this guy is at all times. We can't have him running 'round the country doing as he pleases. It ain't gonna work, that way.'

'We know he'll be in Aberdeen sooner or later.'

'Yeah, but I want him somewhere before that. Anywhere will do. You think he'll go for it?'

'You'll just have to try, otherwise delay the hit in Aberdeen.'

'I guess you're right.' Hassoun checked his watch. 'Let's find out. I'm gonna ring my field operations officer, Parker, and get him to tell Jackson to detrain at the next station. Then you can make those calls.'

'And if he doesn't get off where you tell him?'

'You can make the calls again when he gets to Aberdeen.' Moon shrugged.

Hassoun took out his mobile and pressed a single key. 'Hello, Charlie. It's all RFG here. Good work. Okay, I want you to ring our boy and tell him to hole up at the next station he gets to. Yeah. Tell him there's a problem with Dirlewanger. Yeah. It doesn't matter, just tell him to wait until you call again. Yeah. Okay, goodbye.' He looked back at Moon. 'Done. We'll just wait for confirmation.'

'So, who do you think we're after?' asked Sommer.

'Now, Sergeant, I didn't get where I am today by discussing the Company's work with foreign policemen, even if they are our staunchest allies. Who do *you* think we're chasing?'

Sommer looked at Moon, 'Cos you didn't say the Palestinians, you've got me thinking that they're too obvious.'

Moon looked at Sommer, and then back at Hassoun. 'Is that your way of saying it's not the PLO?'

'I'm not saying anything, Inspector, but there's organisations other than the PLO who might have been in a position to find out about Operation Condor.'

'Like the Russian Interior Ministry, for one,' said Moon.

'Exactly.'

'But why would the Russians give or sell Condor to *al-Qaeda*?' Moon asked.

'Well, that's exactly it, ain't it, Inspector. Not only do we have to find out who was in a position to find out the Stasi's most closely-guarded secret, but also who would pass that on to Mr Bin Laden and his associates. Then we've gotta persuade that gentleman or lady to give us access to their contact. Finding out who sold out the West isn't nearly as important as what we do with him when we got him.'

'It definitely wasn't Berger?' asked Sommer.

'No, we had Berger trussed up like a chicken until . . . ' Hassoun's phone rang and he answered it. 'Yeah. Good. Burr-wick on the Tweed. You sure? Good. Okay, I got it. Goodbye.' He turned back to the policemen, 'He's gonna get off at a place called Burr-wick on the Tweed. You know it?'

'Berwick-upon-Tweed,' said Moon with a trace of sarcasm in his voice, 'is a small town right on the Scottish border.'

'Small?'

'Yeah.'

'Good. I think it's time you made those calls, Inspector.'

Moon nodded to Sommer, 'Grass time, John.' Sommer rose and went to the pay phone. Moon turned back to Hassoun, 'I hope you've at least got an idea what to expect. The Scottish borders aren't the fucking Wild West, you know.'

'Don't worry, Inspector. Let's just say that I'd put a lot of money on one of those phone calls the sergeant is making getting to a particular building in this great city of yours.'

Moon shrugged, 'What are you having?'

'I'll get it.'

'No, this one's on me.'

'I'll try the sirloin steak, even if English beef is undersize and drives you crazy.'

A few minutes later Sommer joined Moon at the bar. 'All done?'

'Yeah.'

'What's the matter, John?'

'I dunno, guv. For some reason I've just got a feeling that this is going to go tits up. I don't trust these Yanks one little bit.'

'Neither do I.'

4

The World Wide Web

Jackson had been in Berwick-upon-Tweed for three days now. On arrival he'd immediately booked into the most expensive hotel in town, the Kings Arms, but it had been a great disappointment, only marginally better than his accommodation in Colchester. The whole town was a disappointment, and after walking around the fortifications and having one of the worst ploughman's lunches he'd ever paid for at the Brewers Arms, he thought he'd exhausted his entertainment opportunities.

Parker had told him to be ready to leave at a moment's notice, so there wasn't a lot he could do. On Friday he'd discovered the restaurant at the Queens Head Hotel, just opposite his own, which seemed the only saving grace in the town. He returned there for dinner that day and spent the evening in Barrels Ale House. It was while he was walking back from the Barrels that he first noticed he was being followed. Whoever it was, was using a team and making a very professional job of it, but Jackson was in no doubt that he was under surveillance. He assumed it was SO12, the CIA, or both, and thought nothing more of it.

By Saturday after breakfast, Jackson had had enough, and hired a bicycle to cycle out to Lindisfarne Island. The trip was a welcome break from the dreary town and although it was cold and windy, the rain mercifully held off. He encountered a few other cyclists and ramblers and he idly wondered how many of them were actually following him, and how many were genuine sightseers or keep-fit enthusiasts. The thought of Moon humping along over rough terrain on a mountain bike just to keep him in sight cheered him up. He might just do it again tomorrow — just to piss the man off.

After returning his bike, showering and changing, he still had four hours to kill before dinner at the Queen's Head again.

He was physically and mentally refreshed from the exertion, and he didn't fancy dulling the feeling by spending the time at the Barrels. His adductor muscle ached, as it always did after exercise, but he was used to the feeling by now. That — and a slightly chipped pelvis — were courtesy of Moon and the one and only time he had worked for SO12. Jackson was thinking about the New England Patriots, the NFL team he followed closely, and wondered if there was any way of getting the latest post-season news. He decided to see if the Kings Arms had internet access for residents.

It did.

★ ★ ★

After visiting both the Patriots and Football League sites, Jackson clicked back on to Google. On a whim he decided to enter 'Dirlewanger' and see what came up. He was no expert on German names, but surely it must be unusual? Most of the results in the first page referred to a 'Dr Oskar Dirlewanger' and Jackson clicked on the first site.

The good doctor was a World War One veteran who spent two years in jail for sex offences in the thirties before being commissioned into the Waffen-SS by an old army colleague in 1940. No doubt considered the best man for the job, he was ordered to raise a penal unit from concentration camp guards who had been court-martialled or arrested. The unit, quite clearly the lowest of the low, spent most of the war hunting partisans and committing atrocities on civilian populations. After a brief period on the front line in 1943, Dirlewanger and his renegades were sent to Poland where, in 1944, they were part of the notorious suppression of the Warsaw Ghetto Uprising. Already a brigadier, Dirlewanger, was — unbelievably — awarded the Knight's Cross and was described as the 'most repulsive figure' to taint its roll. In 1945 he left his unit, fled to Berlin, and was never seen again. Rumour held that he was found by Polish soldiers and beaten to death, although this was never confirmed.

Jackson wondered if the Dirlewanger in

Aberdeen was a relative. He'd never know — and it didn't really matter, because the man was either a conscious or unconscious agent of *al-Qaeda*, and he must die. That was the simple fact of the matter. There was a time when Jackson would have needed to know a lot about a man before he killed him in cold blood. A time when he would have had to be sure that the man was an enemy, or evil. To be sure that killing was the right thing to do.

That time was long gone.

There had also been a time when Jackson had killed whoever his director told him to kill. The dossiers with which he'd been provided hadn't been for the purpose of moral reassurance, but to make the kill more efficient. Jackson hadn't slept so well in those days. But now, it was simple: Dirlewanger was an *al-Qaeda* operative; he must die; Jackson would kill him. It would be a pleasure to strike another blow at the organisation responsible for September 11, Bali, Istanbul, Madrid, the London Underground, and so many other attacks. Which was why Jackson had still slept well after killing Lombard with his wife in the passenger seat of the Smartcar.

Reading about the SS reminded Jackson of the Stasi. In 2004 a mission of his had ended in Berlin. Jackson's boss, Breyten Steenkamp, the Director General of the South African Secret Service, had suggested he take a trip to the Stasi Museum in Normannenstrasse. Steenkamp — along with other senior members of the SASS — had been sent by the African National Congress's Department of Intelligence and Security to the Wilhelm Pieck University in Pomerania, in the German Democratic Republic, in the early eighties. There he had been trained by the Stasi in intelligence and counter-intelligence techniques, before returning to southern Africa to continue the struggle against apartheid.

Jackson had followed his advice and the museum had been absolutely fascinating, a glimpse into a world now gone, a look at perhaps the most frightening organisation ever established. The Stasi made the Gestapo look like Greenpeace. In a country with a population of only seventeen million people, the Stasi employed eighty-one thousand intelligence officers and up to one and a half million informers. In practical terms this meant that just under one in every ten people in the country were employed by the Stasi in either an official or unofficial capacity.

The organisation had been run from the huge complex on *Normannenstrasse* where the museum now stands, with offices and cells in all East German cities, towns, and districts. It was said that nothing happened in East Germany without the Stasi knowing and that they employed any and all methods to keep on top of the population. Looking at the exhibits in the museum, Jackson had believed it. Other than the vast numbers of agents, officers, and informers, the Stasi had monitored the contents of essays written by school children, designed tools to extract mail from post-boxes, used listening devices that plugged into the plumbing, kept samples of the sweat of suspected dissidents, and employed a cornucopia of torture techniques and devices.

The reach and reputation of the Stasi was such that in the late eighties it became an embarrassment to the USSR. This was apparent not only in the role of the Stasi in keeping the Berlin Wall standing longer than the Russians wanted, but also when details came to light that it had been sponsoring Middle-Eastern terrorists in contravention of the wishes of the KGB. When the Wall finally did come down, it was rumoured that the Stasi were well on their way to destroying all their sensitive files, either burning them or pulping them in a machine designed to make animal feed. The KGB was taking no chances, however, and the last month of 1989 saw several high ranking officers sent to East Germany with the sole purpose of retrieving any material considered sensitive by the Russians.

Jackson's thoughts reminded him of Hassoun's comments about the reassembly of Stasi files and he typed another search into Google.

Hassoun had been correct: on the BBC website Jackson found an article dated November 2003 concerning the development of a machine to reassemble the shredded files. Apparently, the German government had employees doing the reassembly by hand and they had already put together half a million pages of documentation. At this rate, however, it would take a further four hundred years to complete the job. The German government was thus in the process of securing fifty million euros in order to fund the development of a machine that could complete the job in five years.

Jackson wondered if Google had anything on Paul Berger, the brigadier who had masterminded Operation Condor. As the name was fairly common Jackson thought he'd enter a search to match 'Paul Berger' with 'South America'. That was what Hassoun had said, that Berger had fled with Operation Condor to South America. He entered the search and waited. There were only a hundred and twenty-seven results, but none of them seemed relevant. He tried again, this time matching 'Paul Berger' with 'escape'.

Four hundred and fifty-three, and still nothing that he recognised. He tried a third time, using 'Paul Berger', 'Stasi', and 'brigadier'.

There was a match straight away at the top of the first page of results. Jackson clicked onto the CNN website: Brigadier Paul Berger, of the Stasi, had committed suicide in February 1991, while awaiting trial for crimes against humanity in the former East Germany.

Jackson leaned back into the chair.

Why had Hassoun lied about Berger? What was the point? Jackson felt a tingle run down his spine and a sudden chill . . . he started when the mobile rang.

It was Parker's phone.

'Ja.'

'We're good to go. Get the hell outta there and get back on the train. I'll see you in your room at the Station Hotel — you can't miss it.'

'I'm booked in?'

'Mr Silver. I'll be in the room.'

Jackson terminated the call.

He was going to have to be a little more careful, this time.

5

Granite Trail

When Jackson had entered his room at the Station Hotel late on Saturday evening, he'd found only an envelope. In it was a brief note from Parker — unsigned — information on Dirlewanger, a map of Aberdeen, and his ID for the next job: John Colt.

Spook humour.

Jackson had added to the Silver and Colt IDs that of 'John Wilké', Wilké being the name he'd used when he'd worked for Moon. What Moon and Sommer hadn't realised was that Jackson had kept the passport he'd been given and used it to obtain a driver's licence and open a bank account after the mission was over. You couldn't be too careful, not when you were dealing with SO12 — or the CIA.

The note from Parker informed Jackson that Dirlewanger would be home alone in the early hours of Monday morning, that his burglar alarm could safely be ignored between midnight and zero-six-hundred on the same morning, and that later that morning Parker was expecting to meet Mr Colt in the departures lounge of Aberdeen Airport no later than nine o'clock.

Jackson had looked through the sparse information on Dirlewanger and registered his address and the fact that he'd been a navy diver in East Germany. In the small South African Navy, divers had been the naval commandos, and Jackson was wary. He missed the Dragunov: it had been the perfect tool for the job.

Twelve hours later Jackson was walking east along Queen's Road, having just left Rubislaw Quarry. He carried a small bag over his shoulder, a tiny digital camera in his left hand, and a booklet entitled *Aberdeen's Granite Trail* in his right. He had just taken about twenty photos of the quarry, the first stop on the trail, and was walking to the second, 50 Queen's Road. Even though he didn't have a laptop, the camera had a powerful zoom and he knew he would be able to bring up details on the display screen that his eyes couldn't see.

The Granite Trail had been a piece of good fortune. Looking for a cover, Jackson had tried the Tourist Information office on the off-chance that it would be open, and found the leaflet. Number three on the trail was Queen's Cross, and on the other side of Queen's Road, behind a hedge and next to the sandstone Rubislaw Church, was Queens Gardens, a row of granite Victorian terrace houses. Dirlewanger owned number eleven, situated between two business premises. Working for Sante Fe, the second largest drilling company in the world, was obviously lucrative.

Jackson had walked from the Tourist Information office west along Union Street, before he'd realised that he'd picked up another shadow. This one was teenage, incompetent, and no doubt a pickpocket. He was not only obvious, but unashamed: even when Jackson made it clear that he'd spotted him, the youth continued to follow. After failing to find a policeman on Union Street, Jackson had led the pickpocket back to the train station. He'd failed to find a policeman there as well, and had gone into the locker-room having made up his mind to give the idiot a hiding and send him on his way. Fortunately for all concerned, the kid had realised he was no longer the predator and when Jackson emerged five minutes later, he was gone.

The trail had been perfect for a second reason as well; not only did it give Jackson an excuse to photograph Dirlewanger's house, but it also took him on a long walk from Union Street to Albyn Place, Queen's Street, and finally Rubislaw Hill. At this time of day, in the wind and intermittent drizzle, there hadn't been many pedestrains around outside of the main shopping areas. Now, as he retraced his footsteps towards 50 Queen Street, he was certain that he was being followed by more than one group.

The first appeared to be the same team that had kept him under surveillance in Berwick and Lindisfarne. There were several of them, they never got too close, and changed appearance and rotated regularly. There was no doubt that they were either Moon or Hassoun's men. Probably Moon's. But there was also another man — on his own, or so it appeared. He was tall and broad with straw-coloured hair, a hook nose, and glasses. He was either an amateur or, more likely, was having to do the job on his own. Jackson suspected the latter and — if that was the case — he was also good, because so far he'd successfully kept out of the all-seeing eye of the camera lens.

Jackson arrived at 50 Queen's Road just as it started raining again. Everything seemed damp in Aberdeen. The air was continually moist, either with water from the sea or from above. Jackson was damp inside his jacket from the long walk, so it made little difference; he just hoped the cloud cover wouldn't ruin the photos. After photographing the front of number fifty, he made a point of back-tracking to find the rear. He took another dozen photos there.

When he went back onto Queen Street

he couldn't see the blonde man anymore, or any of the other group. He arrived at Queen's Cross and spent nearly thirty minutes taking photos there. He took shots of the old bank, the statue of Queen Victoria, Queens Gardens, Rubislaw Church, and Queen Lane North, which was the road running behind the terrace.

Dirlewanger's house, like the rest, had four storeys, one of which was an attic. There was a balcony on the third floor at the front and back, and a skylight in the roof. Parker's reference to a burglar alarm had been accurate. All the houses had long, narrow parking spaces at the rear. The rear of number eleven had a wooden fence obstructing the view of the back door, and no garage. Jackson guessed Dirlewanger would use one of the garages built next to number nine, all six of which had fairly flimsy black wooden doors. The rear of the terrace was overlooked by an ugly concrete office block and a more attractive residential block called Fountainhall, on the other side of Queens Lane North. Jackson thought the residential block might prove troublesome.

He walked back to the roundabout and turned south to make for the next stop, Nellfield Cemetery. Here he caught another glimpse of the blonde man, but it wasn't enough to make sure he could recognise him in a different setting, and once again the man managed to avoid being photographed.

After the cemetery Jackson moved on to Bon Accord Crescent and Square, and then left the trail. There were twenty-four more buildings and statues to see, but they were now all in or around the central shopping area, and would be useless from the point of view of revealing his opposition, if indeed that was what any of the followers were. Besides, his knees were aching from the few miles he'd walked. Too long sitting on the train yesterday, perhaps, or maybe the damp weather.

Jackson walked back up to Union Street and settled down in the Starbucks with a giant Americano. He knew something was amiss. Hassoun's lie and the blonde man if nothing else, but what the hell was really happening? He had no idea. That was the problem. He'd never been particularly bright, and he was well aware of it. Now Lynley, that was a different story. Mrs Jackson was a clever woman. Even without his knowledge of intelligence operations she'd probably have worked out what was going on by now. He missed her.

He turned his mind from pleasant thoughts about his wife back to the problem at hand. He might not be clever enough to work out what Moon and Hassoun were up to, but he was experienced enough to take precautions. The first thing was that Mr Colt would cease to exist the same time as Mr Silver did. Jackson would use the Wilké ID. He'd already drawn out a large amount of cash from the Silver account in Berwick, and he would supplement it with another couple of hundred from the ATM on his way back to the hotel. It was a pity it was a Sunday and he couldn't take more out the bank.

Also, he wouldn't be meeting anyone at the airport tomorrow morning. He'd use a hired car instead, and pay his bill tonight, so that he could leave without checking out in the morning. He'd also decided he was going to need a car for the Dirlewanger job, and he wondered why Parker hadn't provided him with one. So he needed two cars. One SO12 and the blonde man could know about, the other they must not. Just in case. He'd leave the second car a few streets from the hotel, so he could take his surveillance by surprise if necessary. It might not be the best possible plan in the circumstances, but it was the best he could come up with. There was only one problem: he needed to lose his shadows. All of them. If he couldn't do that, there wouldn't be any point.

It would be tough, but Jackson thought he knew how. First, he called up two different taxi companies and arranged two pick-ups. Both were for ten minutes time, one in Union Wynd and one in Union Glen. He hoped the second one would wait. Then he went into the customer toilet, taking his sling-bag with him. He took out a green fleece, a pair of old jeans, and a white baseball cap. He left the bag with his chinos and his suede jacket inside, and disappeared into a part of the building marked 'Staff Only'.

It was a shame, really, because Lynley had bought him the jacket as a present.

★   ★   ★

When *Spy Game* finished on BBC 2 at half-past two on Monday morning, Jackson dressed. He put on soft low-cut black leather hiking boots, dark brown combats, a black polo-neck sweater, and a new black suede jacket. He surveyed the items he'd laid out on the bed: a woollen balaclava, a pair of dark blue police marksman's gloves, the G19 with a silencer and two full magazines at thirty rounds, the Colt .45 with a silencer and three full magazines at twenty-four rounds, a thick leather belt, two holsters for the pistols, three pouches for the extra magazines, an Eickhorn combat knife with sheath, a small black rubber torch, a set of picklocks, his wallet, John Wilké's passport, the keys to a Renault Laguna, the keys to a Volvo S60, and a pillowcase.

The first thing Jackson did was put on the gloves. Each item went into its proper place and he cocked a round into the chamber of each of the pistols. That made thirty-one rounds for the nine millimetre and twenty-five for the forty-five.

He didn't like the forty-five.

He'd only ever fired one once over the years and after discharging two magazines' worth he'd gone back to his nine millimetre. The forty-five might have more of an effect if it struck its target, but it was less likely to do so on anything after the first shot because the recoil was so powerful. Jackson also thought it was too bulky and heavy to conceal comfortably. But he had no other back-up weapon, so there was no choice but to take it. He needed a back-up, especially as he hadn't had the opportunity to fire either pistol yet.

Once everything was either in one of his pockets or attached to his belt, Jackson took the pillowcase and wiped down all the surfaces he'd touched in the room that were likely to yield fingerprints. He'd already disposed of the Dirlewanger notes, the camera, and the Silver and Colt ID documents. He was almost ready. He put his few remaining clothes and toiletries in his sports bag and left it next to the door. He walked out of the hotel into the cold, silent night at just after three o'clock. He crossed the road to the station car park, climbed into the green Renault and started the engine.

6

Collateral Damage

Jackson drove to Queen's Cross and turned right into Fountainhall Road. He glanced up Queens Lane North as he passed: all quiet. He turned left into Desswood Place, and then left again into Forest Road. One more left brought him back into Queens Lane North, which he entered from the western end — the end furthest away from the rear of 11 Queens Gardens. Jackson slowed as he passed Fountainhall flats on the left, and pulled up silently outside the office block, opposite the row of garages between houses nine and seven. He switched off the car, debussed, pushed the door to, and walked into the empty parking space behind Dirlewanger's house.

He approached the green wooden fence silently and stood underneath a hedge hanging down the stone wall which divided eleven and thirteen. All was quiet. There was no sign of any movement in the terraces, or the Fountainhall flats. There was no light at the back of either eleven or thirteen, and the light from number nine cast enough shadow for Jackson to make an undetected entry.

He took his balaclava from his trouser-leg pocket and put it on, covering everything except for his eyes and nose. He looked at Fountainhall, then back at the terrace.

Still complete silence and no visible movement.

He took a deep breath, exhaled slowly, and placed his gloved right hand on the stone wall. He steadied himself with his left on the fence, and heaved over it. He landed nimbly on the other side, crouched low, waited. He forced himself to count ten seconds while he kept dead still.

Silence.

He took off his new jacket, folded it neatly, and placed it behind him, in the corner formed by fence and wall. Underneath the jacket he was wearing both the Glock and the Colt on his belt, along with the three pouches for the spare magazines and the Eickhorn. He checked each was in place: the Glock on his right hip, the Colt on his left, butt forward. He drew the Glock, took its silencer from the same trouser-leg pocket, and screwed it onto the front end of the barrel. Then he waited again, forcing himself to count another ten seconds.

Nothing.

No movement, no sounds. Perfect. Jackson crept forward to the glass doors of a conservatory that had been added onto the back of the house, crouching just underneath the lock. Slowly, centimetre by centimetre, he tried the door . . . it was unlocked.

Always best to try first.

He opened the door gently and quietly, keeping the Glock pointing forward, and his body low . . .

There was a loud thump — the doorframe next to his left cheek crumpled — a splinter buried itself in his forehead — he saw a muzzle flash from inside the room. He fired two shots at the muzzle flash — squeezed through the open door — dived into the conservatory.

Two more silenced shots from inside the house — Jackson fired twice from the floor at the man illuminated by the muzzle flashes.

He heard a cry of pain — a noise upstairs — a crash at the front door — a shout from the back wall: 'Armed police! Drop your weapons! Armed Police!'

Jackson wriggled over to the groaning man and flashed the beam from his torch on him. It wasn't Dirlewanger, it was the blonde man with the hook nose. He'd hit him in the chest and shoulder and he was gasping for breath.

Jackson heard heavy footsteps coming from the front of the house and saw figures approaching the conservatory to the rear. There was no time to think — he must get out immediately.

He pushed to his knees, picked up the blonde man's pistol — a silenced Glock 17 — with his left hand, and fired all of the remaining sixteen rounds through the conservatory windows, aiming low. Glass shattered, dark figures dived and ran for cover. At the same time he stuck his right arm around the doorway into the house and emptied the twelve rounds left in his own pistol down the corridor.

He dropped the Glock 17 and drew the forty-five with his left hand, placing it on the floor in front of him. His right thumb released the empty magazine from the Glock 19; he reloaded, unscrewed the burning hot silencer, picked up the forty-five in his left hand.

Less than four seconds had passed.

He twisted his torso around and sent four shots with the forty-five into the house. He stood, fired a single shot with the forty-five into the casualty's forehead, and charged through the broken conservatory windows. As he came out into the night he fired both pistols simultaneously, briefly glimpsed figures with submachine guns and Kevlar helmets leaping for cover a second time, braced, and hurled himself into the wooden fence.

The fence crumpled, Jackson fell, rolled twice, leapt to his feet, and kept running. He fired the Glock wildly behind him, heard the buzz of a bullet from the police pass close to his right ear, threw the empty Glock down, switched the Colt to his right hand, reloaded. As he reached Queens Lane North, he heard more cracks and muzzle flashes, and saw three figures to his left shooting at him. He kept moving, dived over the bonnet of the Renault, emptied the forty-five at both sets of pursuers, reloaded, took the keys from his pocket, crawled into the car from the passenger side.

Jackson shoved the Colt under his right knee, jammed the key in the ignition, and gunned the engine. Three bullets smashed through the rear right window and the back windscreen. Jackson slammed his foot flat on the accelerator, and the car shot forward.

A police car pulled into Queens Lane North from Fountainhall Road. Jackson wrenched the steering wheel down to the left, hit the oncoming car, and bounced off it onto the curb. The Renault's driver's door flew open as it slid across the pavement, then slammed shut as the car crunched into a parked Opel, bounced off, and continued sliding. The wheels spun loudly on the wet pavement, found traction, and Jackson regained control enough to weave into Fountainhall Road.

He accelerated savagely past Desswood Place, two more side roads, and then slid left into Kings Gate. He pulled up the handbrake, spun the car, waited for it to stop, and opened the door. He knelt next to the door and forced his breathing to slow, holding the Colt steady.

As the first police car came around the corner, he fired two shots at the bonnet, watched it skid and crash into two parked cars, then hurtled into the nearest property, vaulting over a high brick wall.

★   ★   ★

'Jesus fucking Christ!' Moon bellowed, 'don't you dare ask me what the fuck went wrong you arrogant tosspot! What the hell did you do, arm him for a fucking invasion!'

Hassoun was just as angry, but he kept his cool, 'No, I armed him for two jobs. What was I supposed to do, equip the sonofabitch with a goddamn bow and arrow?'

'Well I've got one dead body: gunshot wounds; two CO19 men with gunshot wounds — minor, heaven be praised; and eight other wounded, including two civvies with cuts from shattered windows; and just how the hell . . . '

'The dead body, goddammit, the dead body is the sonofabitch I been tryin' to catch. But he's dead, so he's no fucking good to me.'

'I don't give a flying fuck about your dead body, how the hell am I going to explain this to my governor!'

The two men were in Queens Gardens, outside Rubislaw Church. Moon was pacing up and down outside the church while Hassoun stood with his hands in his overcoat pockets.

'I told you to shoot our boy in the back before he got into the house, but you just couldn't do it, could you? You had to leave him alive so he could waste the sonofabitch I wanted alive, and then escape — to embarrass us all. That's what your famous British fair play has done for us: left my man dead, and got a loose cannon running around who could blow everything sky high. Good work, Inspector, fucking good work.'

Uniformed police and ambulance personnel, along with Crime Scene Investigators and detectives, moved briskly around Hassoun. A small crowd had gathered at Queen's Cross and reporters were flashing cameras, in between trying to enter the police cordon.

'*You* are not in America now, you Yank fuckwit! Coppers in Britain do *not* get away with gunning down people in the back, unlike your lot over there,' he waved his hand at Hassoun. 'I agree it would have been better had he been killed in the cross-fire, but I *cannot* go about giving orders like that. *Collateral damage*, isn't that what you call all the people you kill by accident? Well, if you wanted him dead for definite, *you* should have killed him as soon as that ugly blonde fucker crawled out of the woodwork!' Moon stopped and jabbed his finger at Hassoun.

The American finally lost his temper, 'I would've! I would've if I'd known you were gonna let him waltz out the fuckin' picture. Who trains these guys,' Hassoun indicated two armed policemen standing nearby, 'the goddamn Girl Guides!'

Moon cut him off, 'You piece of shit! Coppers in *this* country have a duty to avoid civilian casualties!'

Sommer was leaning against a metal railing. He looked at the two men, turned a wistful eye to the church, and muttered under his breath, 'I knew this was gonna go tits-up, I just knew it.'

★   ★   ★

Five hours later Jackson calmly climbed into the silver Volvo parked in Dee Street. He was carrying a large order from Burger King in a brown bag, and wore a new set of clothes he'd just bought at Next. The Colt was wedged under his belt, and Moon's mobile was in his pocket, but he had shed all his other equipment. He still had six rounds left in the Colt.

He looked tired, most parts of his body ached in one way or another, and he had a plaster above his left eye where a splinter from the conservatory doorframe had hit him. Otherwise he was unmarked except for a few bruises and grazes under his clothes. He started the engine, tuned the radio to a local station, and turned the car south to head for the A92. He knew exactly what he had to do next because he'd recognised the man he'd killed. When he'd last seen him two years ago, Barry Oosthuizen had been an intelligence officer in the SASS.

7

Wilhelm Pieck Universitat

Jackson knew he had a minimum of eleven hours driving ahead of him. Hopefully that would be enough time to reassess, and perhaps this time he would be able to get to the bottom of Hassoun's game before there were any more unpleasant surprises.

Oosthuizen was either an active or former member of the SASS, the South African Secret Service. The answer to questions must lie there. Somewhere.

Jackson had spent just under five years in the SASS. He'd been recruited from the Security Branch of the South African Police Service — known as the Criminal Intelligence Service — in November 2000, six months after he'd been involved in the high profile trial of a Moslem terrorist leader in Cape Town. Following his initial induction, the following month he had been sent straight to South Africa House in Trafalgar Square to complete his training. The posting was due to the fact that his grandfather was Scottish and that he didn't speak any African languages.

South Africa House was home to the British Isles Station, which covered the United Kingdom and the Republic of Ireland, and was run by Andy Wright, the SIO (Senior Intelligence Officer). He reported to the Assistant Director: the West, then the Director: Rest of the World (as opposed to Africa), Deputy Director General, and, ultimately, Director General Breyten Steenkamp himself. The station was a small one, with only four intelligence officers, seven access and facilities agents, and six intelligence agents. It was officially known as the 'Economic Reconnaissance Department', and Wright's official posting was 'Economic Reconnaissance Manager'.

Jackson had completed his training, and then replaced one of the intelligence officers. On the 12th September 2001 he'd been instructed to report to the FBI headquarters in the J. Edgar Hoover Building on Pennsylvania Avenue, in Washington, D.C. He had been chosen to assist the Americans because of his experience with Moslem extremist groups in South Africa, groups that were linked to *al-Qaeda*. He'd remained in America for the next two years.

In March 2004 he'd been sent back to London where he'd met the new SIO, Anneline Kruis. Under direct orders from Steenkamp, he'd been given a mission which would usually have been carried out by an intelligence agent; like the CIA, the SASS contracted out its dirty work. It was at the end of this mission that he'd spent a weekend in Berlin and visited the Stasi museum. The following month he'd been posted to the South African embassy in Dublin, where his duties for the next year alternated between VIP-protection and more top secret assignments from the Director General.

A year later, Jackson had fallen victim to a political purging of all South African government services, and the circumstances of his resignation — perhaps termination would be more accurate — were not cordial. Kruis herself had escaped the purge, although Jackson didn't believe that the problems he'd had on his final mission had anything to do with her. Like the job that had finished in Berlin, this one had been a direct order from the Director General; and Jackson knew that he'd become a problem for Steenkamp, because he knew too many of the SASS's secrets.

Although Jackson suspected that the SASS had tried to kill him on his final mission, it had been by warning his opposition, not by sending an assassin after him. Oosthuizen, the man Jackson had killed, had been an SASS intelligence officer in 2005. Jackson couldn't be certain that he still was, but if that was the case, there was only one logical explanation: one of the directors of the SASS who had been trained by the Stasi was the man who had handed Operation Condor to *al-Qaeda*.

There was no other way to make sense of recent events. Someone who had been trained by the Stasi at Wilhelm Pieck

University in Rostock had somehow found out about Operation Condor. Someone who had been there in 1988 or 1989. That person had then been given — or stolen — the blueprint for the operation. Jackson couldn't think of a reason Berger — or one of the others — would have passed Condor on to an SASS man, and it would have been a nigh impossible theft, but it was the only way he could make sense of recent events.

Jackson had killed Lombard in Colchester and somewhere between there and Aberdeen, probably while he was diverted to Berwick, the SASS had got on his trail and sent Oosthuizen to protect the second sleeper. Jackson presumed it was an element in the SASS, and not the whole organisation. That was a little too far-fetched. More far-fetched than Stasi sleepers being run by *al-Qaeda*?

Maybe not.

He ran the events through his head step-by-step. Someone in the SASS had sold Condor to *al-Qaeda*. When Jackson had killed the first sleeper, they had sent Oosthuizen to protect their interests by killing him. That meant that the individual in the SASS hadn't just sold the blueprint to *al-Qaeda*: if that person was responsible for protecting the sleepers, he (or she) must actually be working for, or with, *al-Qaeda*.

Fine, no problem.

Oosthuizen had followed Jackson and decided to strike when he came for Dirlewanger . . .

Fine.

Moon and his SO12 team had been following Jackson as well, and had then leapt to his rescue when they heard the shots fired . . .

Problem.

If they had heard the silenced shots, why had they stormed the place? And why had there been so many of them? That hadn't been a surveillance squad, it had been a heavily-armed SWAT team. Had Moon seen Oosthuizen's first shot and thought that Jackson was hit? Jackson doubted it. He'd known it was all wrong the moment he'd recognised Oosthuizen. That was why he'd shot his way out of the house. He hoped he hadn't killed anyone.

So far, it seemed he hadn't. Reports mentioned only one death and several injuries. The death would be Oosthuizen and the injuries . . . well, he hoped he hadn't injured any policemen badly. If he had, it was collateral damage, an unfortunate and unintentional result of his escape.

Shooting his way out had been the only way to ensure he wasn't arrested. He'd deliberately aimed wide of the policemen — which was more than he could say for them once he'd opened fire — but he'd been shooting wildly, trying to get them to take cover rather than follow him. That was why he'd ditched the silencer: he wanted as much confusion and fear as possible; loud, rapid fire to keep police heads down and police bodies behind cover. But it appeared he'd hit more than one of them. He wished them well, but their wounds had been necessary for his freedom. He needed to be free to work out what was going on, and that was exactly what he was doing now. Step-by-step, layer by layer, because he knew he'd never been the cleverest man in the police or SASS.

So: Hassoun and Moon had lied to him. This wasn't just about his brother-in-law, it was more than that. They had wanted *him* specifically, him because . . . it suddenly dawned on Jackson . . .

Berwick.

That was why he'd been left there for two days. So Hassoun could get word to South Africa House that Jackson was the CIA agent killing the sleepers, and then give them enough time to find him. That was how whoever was responsible had got onto Jackson. Hassoun had fed him to them like a sheep to a tiger.

But why? Why did Hassoun need to set Jackson up?

Again there was only one possible answer: he'd wanted to capture Oosthuizen.

Why? If Hassoun and/or Moon had put the word out to South Africa House, why did they need to catch Oosthuizen, or whoever else had been sent to kill Jackson? He couldn't work it out. Why did they need Oosthuizen if they already knew he would be sent to kill Jackson?

Road signs flashed by: Arbroath,

Dundee, Perth, Edinburgh, Wishaw. Jackson crossed the border into England and stopped to refuel somewhere between Preston and Wigan. Reports about the shooting were still coming in, but the suspect was described as 'unidentified' in all of them, and there was no mention of a silver Volvo. It was just after Jackson had joined the M1 that he realised the answer to his own question.

Hassoun and Moon had used him as bait to trap Oosthuizen because they didn't know who the traitor was. But Oosthuizen knew. Hassoun must have guessed that the SASS was involved — that was why he'd selected Jackson. But he didn't know who it was in the SASS, which director. So Jackson's initial thoughts must be correct: it was a rogue element in the SASS led — presumably — by the traitor himself, the man who held the key to Condor. Perhaps Oosthuizen had been part of the group, or perhaps he was just doing his job, like Jackson himself had done in the past.

That was it then.

That was the only answer that fitted the facts he knew. Hassoun was trying to ferret out the traitor, whom he knew to be one of the SASS directors. But he — or Moon — had sprung the ambush too late. Instead of capturing Oosthuizen, they'd given Jackson enough time to kill him. Had they intended to let Oosthuizen kill Jackson first? That was also possible. Likely, even. Once again, it appeared that Jackson knew too much. The optimal result for Hassoun — and Moon — would be Oosthuizen in custody and Jackson six feet under.

But now Oosthuizen was six feet under, not Jackson.

He was glad he'd killed the man; it felt good to have put a spoke in Hassoun's wheels. But, rivalries aside, the traitor still needed finding. And with a little bit more luck, Jackson believed he could do it better and quicker than Hassoun. He scanned the radio's MW bandwidth until he found his favourite station, the Dutch *Arrow Rock Radio*. He was pleased with his reasoning. Others might have reached the same conclusion quicker, but he'd got there in the end. Time to relax for his last few miles.

Jackson dropped the car off in Northampton and spent the night in the Hilton there. The next morning, he was on the five-thirty bus to London.

8

The South African Secret Service

Jackson had known there was a fair chance that Anneline would still be the manager of the Economic Reconnaissance Department in South Africa House. He'd been less certain that she would agree to see him, and even less certain that she'd cooperate with him if she did. Although they'd worked together as an effective team, they'd never been friendly. So far, however, he'd been pleasantly surprised. Not only was she still SIO, but she'd agreed to meet him for a half hour. Which was why he was sitting in The Sherlock Holmes in Northumberland Avenue at midday on Tuesday.

He'd bought a new set of clothes and left a bag in a locker at Victoria Station. There was still no mention of him by name, alias, or description in the news, but Jackson knew that Moon would be looking for him and that it would be better if he didn't find him.

Much better.

Moon was no fool and Jackson knew he'd mobilise the Met sooner or later. It wasn't exactly rocket science: if this was about the SASS, then Jackson would be in or near London, along with about three quarters of a million other South Africans. Unfortunately for Jackson, he didn't know many of them and didn't trust any of them enough to hide him. He wasn't going to book into a hotel either, because the registers would be one of the first places Moon would look. And Moon would be looking for a John Wilké as well as the other names — he and Sommer were thorough.

There'd been half a dozen messages left on the mobile. The first from Moon, angry and threatening. Then one from Parker, and then Hassoun. Another from Moon, more reasonable this time, even conciliatory. Another from Hassoun, and a final one from Sommer. By ten o'clock the message from SO12 and the CIA was the same: come in and talk to us; don't stay out in the cold.

No chance.

The usual haunt of the embassy staff was The Chandos, in St Martin's Lane, but Anneline had opted for The Sherlock Holmes instead. Jackson wondered if she was being naturally cautious because of the circumstances of his resignation, or if there was more to it. Did she know SO12 was after him? It was possible. And there was of course a chance, just a chance, that she was either part of Operation Condor or acting under the orders of someone who was. Which was why Jackson was sitting in an alcove next to the door with the forty-five tucked into his belt. He didn't think he'd need it, but he'd been wrong before. Better to have it and not need it, than need it and not have it.

At twenty-five to one Anneline strode in. Jackson had last seen her almost exactly two years ago. She still had a military bearing about her, and she still looked good. Mid-thirties, close-cropped blonde hair, clean-cut features, erect, confident. She was wearing a black three-quarter length coat over a light blue skirt-suit. There was only one change he could see: she wore a gold engagement ring. Apparently, the ice maiden had relented. She stopped and scanned the room. Jackson stood up, glanced out the door to see if anyone was with her, and came up behind her, brushing her elbow, 'Anneline.'

'Jackson,' she didn't even turn around.

'Perhaps you'd like to buy me a John Smiths while I find us a table.'

'I haven't got time . . . '

'It would look more natural.'

'*Ja*, okay,' she went to the bar, which was busy, while Jackson returned to the table, this time sitting so that he faced the door.

She returned with a pint of John Smiths and a tall glass of Coke. Diet, no doubt, thought Jackson. He remembered she wasn't one for drinking on duty, and when was a spy ever off duty? 'Hello Anneline, congratulations.'

'Congratulations?' She placed the drinks on the table, and took off her coat.

'On your engagement.'

She looked puzzled, then glanced down

at her ring, 'Oh, *ja*, thanks.' She sat down opposite Jackson, 'What's going on?'

'What do you know?'

'No, Jackson, you don't work for me any more. You don't just rock up out the blue and ask questions. *You* tell *me* what's going on or I'm leaving right now.'

'It seems that the SASS are trying to kill me — again.'

'Again?'

'Come on, Anneline, you know what happened in Italy.'

'Hey, I had nothing to do with that.'

'I didn't think you did.'

'If we're trying to kill you, I think I'd know. I *am* still in charge here, you know.'

'You didn't know last time, did you?'

Anneline took a sip of her drink. Jackson noticed her nails were well-manicured, but devoid of any decoration. The ring suited her. She looked at him over the top of the glass. Her eyes were pale blue, like her suit. Like ice. 'You killed Barry, didn't you?'

Jackson made sure no one in their immediate vicinity was listening: '*Ja*, after he tried to kill me.'

'So why do they — we — want you dead?'

'Because I found out something about them . . . about someone in the SASS. It's better if I don't tell you anymore.'

'You're probably right. Who wants you dead?'

'I don't know.'

'Okay, who did you find something out about?'

'I don't know that, either.'

She raised her eyebrows and gave him a look of disbelief. 'How much of a moron do you take me for?'

'No, really, I haven't got a name to the info. That's why I came to see you.'

'Maybe it *is* just better if I tell you what I know.'

'Please.'

'Last Thursday I filed some information that was sent to our office. It was about you.'

'What was it?'

'That you had been in Colchester, were en route to Aberdeen, and were currently in Berwick. It had come via SO12 that morning.'

'What did you do?'

'Logged and filed it. Obviously I thought it was kind of strange — I mean who cares where you are now — but then you know the kinds of thing we get.'

'And then?'

'What do you mean?'

'How did you work out I killed Oosthuizen?'

'Oosthuizen was killed in Aberdeen . . . the message . . . you were there.'

'You don't know anything else?'

'No, of course not.'

'Right, then who sent Oosthuizen?'

'I didn't.'

'The Assistant Director?'

'I don't know?'

'Can you find out?'

'Of course I can, and I'm bloody well going to find out who's been ordering my officers to kill retired agents.'

'I'd like to know. It's very important. All you need to know is that one of the directors wants me dead because of what I know. I don't know how many people know or how many people he has working for him . . . I mean Oosthuizen might just have been following orders. But keep out of it. Take this number,' he gave her the mobile number, 'and ring me as soon as you know who gave the order. The man I'm looking for was trained by the Stasi in East Germany. If Oosthuizen's order didn't come from a graduate of Rostock University, then I need to know who ordered the person who ordered Oosthuizen. Are you with me?'

'I'm *with* the South African Secret Service, and I'm not going to risk any more of its employees, whether they're above or below me in the hierarchy.'

'If I tell you any more, Anneline, you're going to become a potential target yourself.'

'Well I'm not going to betray my country for a former officer who was removed by the government. No way.'

'I'm not asking you to betray your country. The man who gave that order is betraying your country,' Jackson was straining to keep his voice down, 'Come on, Anneline.'

'How's he betraying South Africa?'

'Because he's working for *al-Qaeda*.'

She had been on the verge of getting up, but her muscles relaxed and she had another sip of Diet Coke. She leant forward, her piercing blue eyes boring into Jackson. 'If that's the case, how do *you* know?'

'My brother-in-law left a message for me.'

'The American soldier?'

'*Ja.*'

'He's dead.'

'*Ja*, but I only just got the message.' She didn't look like she believed him. 'Do you know which unit he was in?'

'Marine Corps, wasn't he?'

'Not just the Marines, he was commander of the Anti-Terrorist Brigade. You see?'

Anneline finished her drink slowly. 'If you're telling me that one or more SASS members are working for *al-Qaeda*, then I have to act on that information.'

'Fine, but for both our sakes hold off for a bit. Give me the name of the man who gave the order to kill me, and then give me a fortnight before you do anything. Can you do that for me?'

She stood up and put her coat back on. 'Ja.'

'And the two weeks?'

'Then you'll give me everything you know?'

'Everything.'

She nodded and walked out.

Five minutes later Jackson left the pub. He knew he should probably get as far away from South Africa House as he could, but he decided to have one last look at it, keeping in the middle of Trafalgar Square as he walked up to Charing Cross Road. He'd passed both the embassy and The Chandos when a woman emerged from the pub and turned towards Charing Cross station. A flash of long black hair and pale skin before she turned away and walked towards the Strand. Jackson kept walking — stopped — turned, and followed her. It was risky walking between The Chandos and South Africa House, but he thought he knew the woman . . . and he had an idea.

9

Rosemary Forrester

Four and a half hours later Jackson was following the dark-haired woman down The Broadway. At the New Wimbledon Theatre she turned left into Kings Road, crossed South Park Road, and then turned right into Princes Road. She was carrying a couple of Sainsburys bags in addition to her handbag. Tall, slim, and elegant. She looked as if she was in her late twenties, and Jackson couldn't remember if she was older or younger than that. He'd only seen her in a photograph before, but he rarely forgot a face, particularly one as refined and ethereal as hers.

He was following her along a row of older terrace houses, two storeys with basement and attic. Most of them had different façades and she slowed outside a pink house, next to a pink VW Beetle, and fumbled to open her handbag. Jackson slacked off. She retrieved her keys, stopped at the next house, white in colour, and walked up the steps at front. She unlocked the door and went inside. Jackson glanced at his watch, and kept walking slowly down the road. He gave it a minute, then turned around and returned to the woman's house. He walked up the steps and rapped on the door.

He heard a bolt slide back, and then the door opened slightly, a chain still preventing access. He could see the pale face and straight black hair behind it.

'Rosemary Forrester?'

'Ja?'

'Hello, my name's Jackson. I'm a friend of your brother's and I'd like to talk to you about something.'

Her eyes narrowed. Jackson noticed they were a very dark blue. Her lips were full and slightly parted. She hesitated, 'I wasn't expecting anyone.'

'I'm sorry, I didn't have your number to call.'

'But you had my address?'

'*Ja.*'

'Are you still a policeman?'

Jackson flinched — shocked — 'Er, no, not any more.'

'You'd better come in all the same.' She closed the door, undid the chain, and opened it.

Jackson walked in, wiping his feet on the doormat, 'Those chains are crap, you know.'

'I do, but I don't want to go back to living behind burglar guards again, not ever.' She led him into the lounge, beckoned to him to sit, and sat down opposite him.

There was a small fireplace in the lounge, where a gas fire had been installed. Jackson clasped his hands and tried to put her at ease with a smile, but all he achieved was to exaggerate the scar.

'I didn't know you knew my brother, although I suppose you were policemen together.'

'I'm sorry, Miss Forrester, but how do you know I was a policeman?'

She laughed, revealing straight white teeth, 'Well the same way you know me, of course. And why are you calling me *Miss Forrester*? Your name's Michael isn't it? Does that make you . . . Michael Jackson,' she smiled and waved in apology, 'sorry, I'm not making fun of you!'

It dawned on Jackson. 'Ah, you're thinking of my brother.'

Rosemary Forrester frowned slightly, 'You're Michael's brother? I thought you didn't look quite the same, but then it was a long time ago and . . . ' she touched her left cheek with a fingernail that perfectly matched her lipstick.

Jackson touched his scar and nodded. 'I'll level with you, Miss Forrester, I wasn't a friend of your brother's, I was a colleague. We only worked together once and when we parted I gave him some help. I need help now, and when I saw you leave The Chandos, I wondered if you might return the favour.'

'The Chandos! You've been following me since lunch!' she jumped up.

Jackson raised his palms, '*Ja*, I'm sorry but like I said, I need help.'

Her expression was stern now, but she

sat back down. 'Well I don't suppose there's much I can do now that I've let you in, so you may as well finish your story. Are you really Michael's brother?'

'Ja, how did you know him?'

'Just from the gym. Remember Health & Racquet in La Lucia?'

'Ja.'

'How is he?'

'He's dead, Miss Forrester. My brother was murdered and your brother was called in to work the case. That's how I met him. He solved it. He was good.'

'I'm sorry, I liked Michael. But wait a bit . . . his name wasn't Jackson, it was Baston. Are you . . . '

'I changed my name after his murder. I'm Jackson now.'

'My name's Rosemary.' Jackson nodded. 'My brother solved Michael's murder?'

'Ja, and I did do him a favour, but the truth is we didn't get on, and you're under no obligation to help me.'

'What do you want?'

'I need a place to stay for three nights.'

'Are you short of money?'

'No, I can't use a hotel because the

92

police are looking for me.'

She raised her eyebrows, 'Don't you think you should try lying to me, as this brutal truth isn't exactly putting me at ease?'

'I work for the South African Secret Service,' he obliged.

'Really?'

'Really. I left the police seven years ago and transferred over.'

'Then how come they don't put you up in a . . . safe-house . . . or something?'

'Again, the police. I need to go to ground somewhere that has no connection to my life or the South African embassy. I saw you walking out the pub, and thought it was the perfect opportunity — *if* I could persuade you to help me.'

'How did you recognise me? I only knew Michael casually, and I'm sure we've never met.'

'We haven't, I recognised you from a photo.'

'You must have a very good memory.'

'You have a memorable face.'

Rosemary smiled, 'If you followed me

from Trafalgar Square, you'll know I work for Wellbeloved, Sim & Murray solicitors. I'm a legal secretary and I can't exactly afford to be found harbouring a felon.'

'You won't be. I'm not a felon, but Special Branch are looking for me. But I don't want you to feel threatened. If you say no, I'll disappear now and you'll never see me again.'

She was quiet for a while, then smiled again, 'You must be good at disappearing as well as remembering.' Jackson grinned. 'Okay, you can stay for a bit. I moved in here after my divorce and I live on my own, which probably suits you all the more if you're going to hide here. Is that all your stuff?' she pointed at his sling-bag.

'*Ja.*'

'You travel light. Do you want a drink . . . '

★ ★ ★

Anneline didn't call. Parker did, three times; Sommer, twice; and Hassoun, once. They all left the standard message about getting in touch and bringing Jackson in. He wondered if Anneline had changed her mind, or been indiscreet and put the traitors on their guard. There was nothing he could do, except sit and wait.

Forty-six hours after he'd seen Anneline, she rang and left a number and a time. Two hours later Jackson rang the number from a callbox on The Broadway. It was another public phone.

'Ja?'

'You're not using anything near Trafalgar Square are you? SO12 might have bugged nearby pay phones.'

'Of course I'm not. Do you want the name or not?'

'Who is it?'

'Konnie Raymond.'

'Director Global and Transnational?'

'Was. Now Deputy Director General: Rest of the World.'

'Stasi-trained?'

'Ja.'

'When?'

'1983 and 1988.'

'He was at Rostock University in 1988?'

'Ja.'

'Right. Now just give me two weeks before you do anything.'

'There's one more thing I thought you'd like to know?'

'What?'

'He flew out to Barbados on Saturday for a two week holiday. He's staying in Long Bay.'

'Long Bay?'

'Ja.'

'Thank you, you've . . . '

She'd already put the phone down.

Jackson didn't know much about Konnie Raymond, except that he was coloured, was one of the founding directors of the SASS, and was a crony of the Director General. And now he was a traitor to his country, to the West, and to anyone who tried to protect the innocent from terrorism. Jackson had a vague memory of him being ex-Pan-Africanist Security Service, the intelligence agency that had spearheaded the Azanian People's Liberation Army terror attacks right up until April 1994. He'd met him once or twice, but only briefly.

It was, of course, possible that the conspiracy ran higher. It was even possible that Raymond was in league with Breyten Steenkamp. Jackson would have to find out. But he could only do that by renewing his acquaintance with Mr Raymond. And Raymond was in Barbados. Jackson wasn't sure if that made it better or worse. He was still in the phone booth when his mobile rang: Hassoun's phone. Jackson decided to answer this time.

'Ja.'

'I'm glad I've got hold of you at last, Mr Jackson. I was concerned for your well-being after the misunderstanding on Monday morning.'

'I'll meet you at midnight. Just you. No SO12, no Parker, no agents.'

'That's no problem. Where?'

'In London.'

'That's a pretty big old place, Mr Jackson, how about I choose somewhere comfortable?'

'I'll ring you half an hour before on this number.' Jackson clicked the phone off, left the phone booth and headed for the tube station.

⋆ ⋆ ⋆

When Rosemary came home on Thursday evening Jackson had prepared them a meal of salmon steak, mushrooms, tomatoes, and chips. He wasn't sure if she'd approve of his simple fare, but she did. He drank grape juice instead of wine. When they'd finished the meal and the chocolate dessert he'd bought, they sat back with their glasses. Rosemary was smiling, 'You're a very strange house-guest, Jackson, but no trouble at all.'

'Thanks,' he smiled. 'I'm leaving tonight so this is as good a point as any to thank you for everything.'

She was surprised, 'So soon?'

'*Ja*, I've been lucky enough to find out what I want quickly.'

'So what now? You're disappearing?'

'Just lying low for a little while. By the time I surface Special Branch will have forgotten all about me. You might not want to mention me to your brother, by the way.'

'Why?'

'We didn't part on very good terms.'

'He lives in Australia now. I'll just tell him I bumped into you in The Chandos when I speak to him.'

Jackson smiled, 'Okay. I'll be gone about ten o'clock. I've one more favour to ask . . . '

'*Ja*, what is it?'

'I'd like to steal your car.'

'You're asking permission to steal my car!' she burst out in laughter, rocking forward on the settee.

'*Ja*.'

'Well what if I say no.'

Jackson shrugged, 'I'll have to steal someone else's.'

She was still laughing, 'Then I suppose you'd better steal mine after all. Am I likely to get it back?'

'*Ja*, if everything goes to plan I'll leave it somewhere safe; locked, and with the keys under the driver's seat. It should be back with you in a couple of days, but I'd rather you didn't report it until you leave for work tomorrow morning.'

'You *are* joking aren't you?'

'Er . . . no,' Jackson realised the idea was a little out of the ordinary, but he didn't think it was all that strange: he did need a car.

'Seeing as you've asked so politely, you may steal my car with pleasure,' she left the lounge and retrieved the spare key, which she threw in his lap. 'There you are,' she said as she sat down, still giggling.

'Thanks,' Jackson looked at the keys, attached to a Volkswagen key-ring, 'What's so funny.'

She started laughing again, harder this time, doubling over. 'It's the VW outside . . . the pink Beetle!'

Jackson's scar twitched. It was just what every ruthless assassin needed to get him from one murder to the next. His scar twitched again and he laughed, and Rosemary laughed with him, and it felt good. He realised that he hadn't laughed since before Lynley had left for work last Monday morning.

10

Midnight in Chelsea

At twenty-three-thirty-five Jackson had rung Hassoun and told him to meet him outside a pub called Partridges on Kings Road in Chelsea. Between the pub and King's Walk shopping centre there was a small, circular park enclosed by low metal railings. Jackson would be waiting at the railings.

He was in two minds as to whether it would be safer to arrive first or second. He was also in two minds as to whether there was any advantage to be had in meeting Hassoun. The disadvantage was obvious: there was a risk, a big risk, of capture. The advantages were less tangible, and less likely to materialise. Jackson wanted to find out if Hassoun knew about Raymond yet. If he did, Jackson would have a tough time going after the man. If not, there was a good chance Jackson could find him in Barbados. Even if Hassoun was willing to trade information, he would probably lie to Jackson. Maybe he shouldn't bother at all . . .

Jackson decided to arrive first, and was in position ten minutes after he'd phoned Hassoun. Partridges and a restaurant called Jigsaw were directly ahead of him. Between the two establishments was a narrow walkway to the *al fresco* dining area at the rear of Jigsaw. Two low metal gates blocked access and the dining area was enclosed by a high metal railing, behind which was Cheltenham Terrace, a narrow road forming a T-junction with Kings Road. Behind Jackson was a tidy plaza, leading to the shopping centre about forty metres away. Kings Road was on his right, the park on his left. He had chosen this site earlier in the day: it offered good visibility and an escape route which wasn't too obvious.

Jackson leaned back against the railing and looked over at the shopping centre through the light drizzle that had started about ten minutes beforehand. There were a few people walking about, and some groups leaving pubs, but not enough to cover a clandestine approach. He had told Hassoun to go to the *Al-Dar* Lebanese Restaurant on the corner of Kings and Lincoln, and then cross Kings Road to meet him in the plaza. He'd warned him that if he used another route, was accompanied, or more than five minutes late, they would not meet. He had also led Hassoun to believe that he would be arriving before Jackson, and that he would be under surveillance. Which was why Jackson had decided to arrive first.

At two minutes past twelve Jackson saw Hassoun standing outside *Al-Dar*. He stood on the pavement and made himself visible, as instructed. Then he saw Jackson, crossed the road, and walked over to him. Jackson took a couple of steps towards him and then waited for him, scanning all around to see if there was anyone else with him. When Hassoun was a couple of metres away Jackson put his hand up, 'That's far enough Hassoun.'

'No problem, Mr Jackson,' Hassoun

took his hands out of his overcoat pockets and held them palms up. Jackson nodded, and Hassoun continued, 'I hope I can set your mind at rest and put this little misunderstanding to an end. I've already squared away everything with Inspector Moon and the local cops, so you shouldn't concern yourself with any of that.'

'I'm not,' Jackson scanned his surrounds again, always keeping Hassoun in at least peripheral vision.

'I ain't gonna bullshit you, Mr Jackson. We underestimated you and we did you a disservice. Moon told me you were the perfect patsy, so I set you up. For that, I apologize, but now that you've shown us all your true calibre I want you to do a job for me and I'll pay you what you're worth.'

Jackson's scar twitched and he half-smiled with irony, 'You admit to setting me up, trying to kill me in fact, and then offer me a job?'

'You're wrong there, Mr Jackson, we may have set you up but we did our best to keep you alive — that's what all those

SWAT guys were doin' at Queens Cross, keepin' you alive.'

'Before I consider any job offer I want to know everything — now.'

'Not a problem. Why don't we get outta this shit British weather and go for a drink, I saw a late night bar up the street . . . '

'Talk.'

Hassoun shrugged again, 'If that's what you want.'

'Talk.'

'You're gonna be surprised at how little I lied to you, Mr Jackson. I ain't gonna repeat myself about how we found out about Condor, because it was all true. There was only one thing I didn't tell you. There were five people who knew about Condor, not four, and that mystery fifth guy sold out, not Brigadier Berger.'

'Berger committed suicide in 1991.'

'That's right. Berger, the Condor mastermind, committed suicide while on trial for crimes against humanity. No doubt he was scared that Condor would be discovered, as well as whatever other dirty tricks he'd been up to. Mielke, the bastard who ran the Stasi and terrorised Germans for forty years, died in an old age home in May 2000. I hope the son of a bitch is still turning over in hell. Do you see where I'm going with this, Mr Jackson?'

'Schellong and Kaminski?' Jackson was intrigued, but maintained his vigilance nonetheless.

'Right. Number Five decided that it wasn't safe to revive Condor until he was the only man who knew about it. Needed to remove the competition, if you like.'

'So he killed Schellong and his family in the car crash.'

'We're pretty sure of that, yeah. We're also pretty sure that he removed Colonel Kaminski from play at the end of 2000. With Mielke dead, that was his last loose end tied up. And *you know* the South African Secret Service has been involved in assassinations, don't you?'

'How did you know it was a South African?'

'Process of elimination. The information we received suggested a time period within which Berger could have passed on the protocols. Put together with what was happening in the Eastern Bloc at the time we were pretty sure that it was one of five people who were at Rostock University in the second semester of eighty-eight. There were three South Africans, a Zambian, and an Angolan. The Angolan was killed just after he returned home, the Zambian died of AIDS in 1999, and what are we left with?'

'Three South Africans.'

'All of whom were or are high ranking members of the South African Secret Service.'

'Who are they?'

'Glen Madondo, Konnie Raymond, and Reginald Mybergh. Ring any bells.'

'*Ja*, Mybergh is a police commissioner, and Raymond and Madondo are directors in the Secret Service.'

'Exactly.'

'Which one is it?'

'We don't know and that's what I'm doin' standing here talking to you again. The odds are against Mybergh, although it's not impossible because he supervises overseas work, but we reckon it's either

Madondo or Raymond. And I want you to find out which.'

Jackson glanced around again, and shook his head, grimacing, 'You are unbelievable.'

'Don't kid me, Mr Jackson, I know you hate those guys. They tried to kill you in Italy for no reason other than that you'd been around too long. I know all about that.'

'I thought you might.'

'Fucking-A, I do. The mission was a joint CIA-SASS one. The SASS were gonna kill someone we'd been wanting rid of for a long time. They sent you on your own thinking that the mark would take you out. As a back-up plan they had the Italian police searching for you as a dangerous terrorist. Do you know there was a special *Carabinieri* unit scouring the Alps with orders to shoot you on sight?'

'I didn't, but I believe it.'

'So I'm offering you a chance to get back at those bastards. They try to kill you for nothing and you're just gonna live and let live! Come on, Mr Jackson, there's an opportunity here for a man like you.'

'No.'

'You gotta be kidding.'

'The thing is, I changed sides once before; when the Security Branch became the Criminal Intelligence Service. One year I was hunting Stasi-trained spies, the next I was working for one. As time went on I began to doubt whether or not I'd done the right thing,' he shrugged his shoulders. 'So I'm not going to change sides again. Nice try, though.'

'I don't wanna hear that. You goddamn killed that stupid sonofabitch Oosthuizen and put us back to square one! Come on, Mr Jackson, if you won't do it to get back at your enemies, do it out of a sense of dooty. We gotta find out who sold us all out to *al-Qaeda*.'

'You're the CIA, you do it.'

'We need an inside man, and you're it. It's not just about finding the traitor, you know, this is bigger than Madondo and Raymond. It's about using the treacherous bastard to get access to *al-Qaeda*. This could be the break we been waiting for.'

'I'm leaving now,' said Jackson, taking a step around Hassoun.

The American put his hands up to stop him, 'No you ain't,' his smile was malicious.

Jackson stepped back and glanced around him. There were two men jogging through the park towards him, two coming from the shopping centre behind him, and one from *Al-Dar* across the road. Jackson deliberately relaxed his shoulders and smiled his resignation at Hassoun. But he was watching the man crossing Kings Road. It was Parker and he would be with Hassoun the quickest. As soon as Parker had crossed Jackson said, 'Why fight it, if the CIA want me, they'll get me?'

Hassoun smiled, 'Now that's more like it . . . '

He never finished the sentence because Jackson whipped out the Eickhorn pressed against the small of his back and plunged it into Hassoun's left thigh.

Hassoun screamed and clutched his leg.

Jackson left the knife in the wound and

bolted past Hassoun. Parker sprinted past Jigsaw to cut him off, but missed. Jackson vaulted the two small gates between Jigsaw and Partridges, jumped up onto an *al fresco* table and hauled himself over the railings. As he lifted himself up he kicked the table away. He fell heavily onto Cheltenham Terrace, saw Parker trying a more difficult route over the railings, and sprinted left down Kings Road. Seconds later he cut into Sloane Avenue, then Draycott. He lay low for a few seconds, saw no pursuit, and climbed into Rosemary's pink VW.

So Hassoun didn't know about Raymond. Not yet, anyway. Which gave Jackson some time. But would it be enough?

★   ★   ★

Six hours later Jackson left the car parked safely in the centre of Beddgelert, in Snowdonia National Park. It was still drizzling when he found the station there.

111

11

Ceade Mille Failte

Jackson didn't waste any time when he arrived in Dublin by bus at fifteen-twenty-eight on Friday. He went straight to the General Post Office, the one with the bullet holes in O'Connell Street, purchased envelopes and packaging material, and found the nearest public toilet. When he was finished he went back into the post office and dispatched three tightly-wrapped packages to Mr John Wilké, c/o the Sea Breeze Beach Hotel in Christ Church, on the south coast of Barbados.

Then he took a taxi straight to Phoenix Park in the hope he might find Mary Moroney in her office.

Mary was a contact from Jackson's time doing VIP protection in the South African embassy in Dublin. She was a *ban garda* (policewoman) in the Special

Detective Unit of *An Garda Síochána*, Ireland's national police service. The 'Guardians of the Peace', as the literal translation from the Gaelic reads, have their national headquarters in a complex in Phoenix Park, west of Dublin City. The Special Detective Unit performs a variety of duties, from VIP protection and robbery decoy to an SO12 and anti-terrorist role, as well as including the Emergency Response Unit, a Special Forces hostage rescue team.

As an inspector, Mary was second-in-command of the VIP protection squad. At thirty-five, she had done well for herself, being one of only eighteen female officers in a force of nearly twelve thousand police personnel. Like all of Ireland's plain-clothes police, she was always armed on duty.

Jackson knew that if she had the weekend off she'd be on her way to Galway already. She lived in the city of her birth with her husband, Larry Jennings, an Englishman from Coventry. Larry was a former Royal Engineers bomb disposal expert who now worked

113

for a private company defusing bombs in the less salubrious parts of the world. He had spent six or more months of each of the last three years on contracts in the Middle East.

Jackson was instructed to wait in the reception area of the police complex. He gave his real name, and hoped for the best. There was always a possibility that Moon had informed both the Police Service of Northern Ireland and the *Garda* that he was looking for Jackson-cum-Wilké. If he had, it would be the Special Detective Unit of the *Garda* that would have received the information, so Jackson would soon know one way or the other.

Mary was in, but Jackson was told to wait where he was; she would come down and fetch him. He was not given a visitor's pass, which he thought strange. He wondered if he shouldn't just leave right now.

Mary arrived about ten minutes later. She was short with shoulder-length black hair and a voluptuous build understated by her smart pants-suit. 'Jackson! Hello, how are ya!' She had a small sports bag in one hand and hugged him with the other.

'Hello Mary, it's good to see you.'

'I'm just leaving for the weekend, so we'll go somewhere and have a drink, aye?'

'Fine,' Jackson smiled back. He'd always found her gently lilting accent charming.

She rented a small house in Castle-nock, near the ring road, as a digs in Dublin. Jackson squeezed into her metallic gold MX convertible in the police car park.

'Where's Lynley?'

'At home. I'm actually here on business, not pleasure.'

'I thought you were retired, mind?'

'I keep trying to retire, but it's harder than you'd think.'

They pulled out of the police complex and turned north-west. 'Where are you staying just now, in town?'

'Nowhere, actually, that's one of the reasons I came to see you.'

'You mean it wasn't just for my charming company?'

'I said *one* of the reasons. But the truth is I need a place to stay and I'm not sure if a hotel would be a good idea.'

'Why not?'

'Up until Monday I was contracting for SO12.'

'Again? I thought you said that was all over?'

'It's complicated. Anyway, as of Monday I've been contracted by the CIA and SO12 aren't too happy about it. I thought there was a possibility they might've even got in touch with the SDU. I was half expecting your Emergency Response boys to swoop while I was waiting for you.'

She laughed, 'No, I haven't seen anything about you.'

'That's a relief. Anyway, I need a place for the night if that's alright?'

'Of course. Where's your bags?'

Jackson pointed at the sling-bag at his feet, 'That's it.'

'Oh, are you in trouble?'

'A little, but I'm on the first available flight to Barbados tomorrow so I'll be out of your hair completely. If you do get questioned, I'd rather you didn't mention

Barbados. I've just told you I'm flying to Johannesburg tomorrow.'

She glanced at him, 'Sounds a bit much for a retired spy. I won't ask why you're going to the Caribbean.'

'Good. Anyway, that's it. If you need to shoot off, I'd appreciate it if you could let me in to your place first.'

'No, I'm not in any rush. Lawrence is in Iraq at the minute, so I'm only going back to see mum and dad. If you fancy a drink or two I might stay. I can drive back tomorrow morning, I'm only back at work Monday week.'

'*Ja*, that would be great.'

'Good. We'll go back to mine and then go into town. I'll take you to O'Donoghues. That was your favourite, wasn't it?'

'To be sure,' replied Jackson.

While Mary showered and changed Jackson phoned Dublin airport information for flights leaving on Saturday. There was one flying out at seven thirty and arriving in Bridgetown via Florida at half-twelve Caribbean time. It would do. He asked Mary if she wouldn't mind taking him shopping for clothes before they went to the pub and she replied that she really was pleased to see him.

★ ★ ★

By half-six they were sitting at a tiny table in O'Donoghues on Merrion Row. Jackson wasn't a big fan of Guinness, but he had a pint in front of him with a Jameson chaser to ease it down. When in Dublin ... He also had four bags from various clothes shops in St Stephen's Green. Mary had a small bag herself. It was while they'd been shopping that another idea had occurred to him. 'Seeing as this is the place for a bit of *craic*, I'm going to tell you a story.'

'Will I like it?' her smile showed very white teeth.

'No, but you won't be bored.' He proceeded to tell her all about Condor and the events leading up to his arrival at her office. He told her everything except the shooting at Queens Cross and the stabbing in Chelsea.

'So you're not working for the CIA anymore?'

'No.'

'So why are you going to Barbados?'

'To find Raymond.'

'What for?'

Jackson shrugged, 'To kill him of course.'

'What about the CIA taking him alive so they can turn him against *al-Qaeda*?'

'The CIA have spent six and a half years trying to turn *al-Qaeda* operatives against their masters without success. Besides, Raymond won't be in their inner circle. He's no doubt been well paid for his treachery, but they won't trust him any more than I do.'

'You're probably right. But why not just let the CIA pick him up anyway?'

'Because once they pick him up he'll be safe.'

'Why do you want him dead?'

'Because he killed my brother-in-law.'

'You were close?'

'No, I only met him three times and I thought he was an arrogant prick, not to mention a bad husband.'

Mary smiled, 'So why are you going to all this effort to avenge him?'

'Because he's family. Because I promised Lynley. And because her sister and mother will be happy when I eventually tell them.'

'I'm not even going to try and talk you out of it seeing as you've obviously made your mind up already.'

'Well I'm going to try and talk *you* into something.'

'Me? What are you on about?'

'Come with me to Barbados.'

'And help you murder Raymond! Have you lost the plot?'

'No, no, of course not,' Jackson lowered his head and raised his palms in a placatory gesture. 'Just come and stay with me, for cover. I won't even tell you what I'm doing if you don't want.' She looked anything but convinced. 'I thought about it today, while we were shopping. Nobody notices couples, but if I'm correct Barbados is a small island. A man with this,' he touched his scar, 'snooping around might attract attention. I don't want Raymond put on the alert or — even worse — trouble getting back.'

'And you want me to leave with you tomorrow?'

'*Ja*, I'm paying. Hassoun left my expense account open as a show of good faith. I removed a considerable amount of money from it on Thursday afternoon. A week in the Caribbean, my treat, how could you say no?' He wasn't quite pleading. but he was getting there.

'If I say no you'll go anyway, won't ya.'

'*Ja*.'

'Aye, well, I suppose someone's got to look after your arse. If I get a suntan while I'm there, then that's just my well-deserved good fortune. What time do we leave?'

'First thing.'

'Then we'd better get back and do some packing.'

'*Ja*, I've a few calls to make.'

★   ★   ★

Jackson made his last call five minutes before midnight. It was much earlier in

Virginia Beach, Virginia, on the American east coast.

'Hello?'

'Jay, Jackson. How are you?'

'Looking forward to seeing you and the lovely Mrs Jackson in a couple months. How are *you*, son?'

'I need help with something.'

'Well don't beat about the bush, son, just tell me what you need. If I can do it, I will; otherwise, you're on your own.'

'Have you got any contacts in Barbados?'

'Contacts of what sort?'

'I'm doing a job and I'm going to need some equipment.'

'I thought we were both retired. Don't you fall off mountains for kicks these days?'

'It's been harder staying retired than I anticipated.'

'Okay, so you want a man that can get you some hardware in Barbados?'

'Ja.'

'Where will you be staying?'

'I'm not a hundred percent sure yet.'

'I don't think it matters much, it's a

miniature island.'

'You've got a contact?'

'Not there, but I know some boys on the Virgin Islands, where you got married. I'm sure they can put me in touch with someone. Give me a couple days.'

'I'll call you on Sunday.'

'Do that,' and he was gone.

Jackson was alone in the lounge, Mary having gone to bed already. He yawned, looked at his watch, set the alarm for five o'clock, switched off the light, and found the spare bedroom.

12

Jewel of the Third World

'Hello?'

'Jay, Jackson; any luck?'

'Yeah, I know a guy who knows a guy who knows a guy who might be able to help.'

'Good.'

'His name's Davis Teacher, lives in Kensington, in Bridgetown. You copy?'

'*Ja*.'

Jay gave Jackson a Bajan mobile number, 'Tell him José gave you his number. Copy?'

'*Ja*, thanks. I really appreciate it.'

'No problem, you just make sure you're alive and well when I come to visit you in England. You copy?'

'I'll be there.'

'On second thoughts, if you ain't there, send Mrs Jackson anyway and we'll see if this old dog's still got any life in him.'

Jackson laughed, 'Well I'll just *have* to be there in that case.'

'Good,' Jay was gone again.

Jackson dialled the number he'd been given.

'Yeah?' The accent was more American than Bajan.

'A man called José told me Mr Teacher could help with a security problem I've got.'

'What's your problem, man?'

'I've lost my iron.'

'What you lookin' for?'

'Another iron. It was a number nine.'

'Wha's your name and where are you?'

'Jackson. I'm at the Sea Breeze, Christ Church.'

'I have a man pick you up in half-hour. Man's name is Marmaduke. He be drivin' a taxi, a white Merc. You wait outside, you bring plenty o' Mr Barrows. Understand?'

'Perfectly.'

Teacher — if it was him — terminated the call. Errol Barrow, in addition to being an RAF officer during the Second World War, was the first Prime Minister of Barbados, and adorned the fifty dollar bill — the largest Bajan currency note.

Jackson was sitting on the king size bed in the second-floor room overlooking the Caribbean Sea. He'd been lucky enough to get a room without booking, although he couldn't understand why. March was supposed to be the coolest month of the year and yet he was sure, with the humidity, it was at least thirty degrees. There were clouds in the sky, but they were white, and the sun was bright.

Mary was reclining on a lounger on the balcony. Last night it had been so warm that Jackson had slept out on the lounger with only a sheet to cover him. The place was fantastic. Peaceful, balmy, idyllic. Palm trees, mahogany trees, fragrant flowers, fine white sand, and a clear blue sea with gentle waves lazily lapping at the shore. Mary was wearing a bikini and a very large pair of sunglasses. Her naturally dusky skin had already started to tan. Jackson followed the curves of her flesh from her shoulders down to her legs and felt the first stirrings of desire.

Quickly, he got up and put on his shirt and sandals.

He checked his money: a thousand dollars, equivalent to about five hundred American. He put them all in his wallet and slipped a lock-knife with a six inch blade into his pocket. It was all he'd been able to get so far, but then it was difficult to conceal anything bigger when you were only wearing shorts and a T-shirt. 'I'm going out for a bit,' he said to Mary, 'I've got my key in case I'm a while and you're out.'

'Who's this Jay, is he a friend of yours?'

'*Ja*, I met him when I worked with the FBI. He's retired now. He comes out to stay in the Yorkshire Dales every May so I still see him at least once a year.'

'Reliable?'

'Absolutely.'

'Will you be long?'

'I hope not.'

'I'll wait here until lunch then.'

'Bye.' Jackson checked at reception again, just in case his parcels had arrived, although he wasn't expecting them for a few days yet. They hadn't. He walked out of the hotel and sat on a low wall, thankful for his sunglasses.

There were a group of about six local men operating a vending stand about twenty metres away. He hoped they would ignore him. Jackson had read that back during the Cold War — when the world was divided into West, East, and Third — Barbados was hailed as an example of what all developing nations (as they were now called) could aspire to. So far, despite the scenery, he hadn't been particularly impressed. He'd already been offered drugs four times, twice each cannabis and cocaine. People usually didn't bother to approach him. In fact, in the last twenty-two years he'd only been approached twice. Until yesterday. Oistins to the east, and St Lawrence to the west, were both reputed to be full of drugs for anyone who was — or wasn't — interested. And their room service break-fast hadn't materialised this morning, either.

True to form, one of the locals sidled up to him. Before he could get to whichever particular product he was peddling, Jackson declined. The man sucked at the back of his teeth and swaggered back to his colleagues. They made a few loud comments and gave him some dirty looks, but soon lost interest when a young woman jogged by.

An hour and ten minutes later a white Mercedes taxi pulled up sharply, showering Jackson's sandals with gravel. He stood.

A tall black man with a flabby torso and buttocks and skinny arms bounced out of the car. He had short peppercorn hair and a razor-thin moustache. 'You Jackson?'

Jackson nodded, 'Marmaduke?'

'Tha's Misster Marmaduke to you, blud. Ge' in.'

As soon as Jackson had climbed in the rear door on the passenger's side the car pulled off with a loud wheelspin.

'Man's takin' you te Bridgetown see Misster Teach. You got Misster Barrow in your pocket, blud?'

'Ja.'

'Then we get along jus' fine.'

They had only been driving along the

main road to Bridgetown for ten minutes when Marmaduke turned left, into a run-down residential area. He said nothing, but Jackson could see the man was watching him out of the corner of his eye. Jackson slipped his right hand into his pocket, slowly. He opened the lock-knife and gripped it, keeping it inside the pocket, out of sight.

A minute or so later Marmaduke pulled up just before a house on the left where a woman was running some kind of takeaway service from a small veranda. There were two children and one customer with her.

Marmaduke jerked up the handbrake, not bothering to disengage the ratchets. 'Man's goin' grab pot o' Bajan soup.' He shuffled his bulk around, but instead of opening the door he spun around to Jackson, pointing a Beretta 92 Centurion 9mm pistol at him.

'I smell bacon, blud. You a pig?'

Jackson sighed, 'No. Are you interested in Mr Barrow or not?'

'Man comes to buy gun, man got no gun. So maybe I just take Mr Barrow and keep your iron. Then evaht'ing cook n curry.'

'If you're going to mug me, then fucking get on with it. Otherwise, I'll buy that nine-iron you're pointing at me.'

The woman on the veranda had two more customers. Marmaduke and his Beretta were in plain sight, but everyone ignored the Mercedes completely. Marmaduke sucked his teeth, 'This, man's iron. Iron for you in de boot. Eight hunnerd dollars.'

'Fuck off. What make is it?'

'Big silver motherfucker. Colt Python with a faw-inch barrel.'

'I asked for a nine-iron. How about yours?'

'No way. You take the Colt or you leave it. Either way you give man eight hunnerd dollars.'

'Four, and I want at least twenty-five rounds with that.'

'You dissing man wi' bullshit price,' he waved the Beretta, 'you try again, bludklaat.'

'Five hundred or you'll just have to mug me. Take it or leave it, fat boy.'

Marmaduke sucked his teeth louder this time. 'Now you dissing man big-style. I had people killed for less than tha'. Man's not fat, he well-built. Ladies like a good build.'

'Five hundred.'

'Six hundred and you choose yo' ammo. Man got evaht'ing you can buy, evahting.'

'Like what?'

'Full mehtal jacket, hollow point, hydrashock, disintegrator, evaht'ing.'

'What about eliminator?'

'Tcha, wassa' man?'

'Red plastic tip.'

'You makin' dat shit up. Six hunnerd and you choose ammo. Fifty bullets if you like.'

'Done.'

Marmaduke held out his left hand, squeezing it past his stomach, 'Give man money.'

'You put the nine-iron away, show me the goods, then I'll give you the money.'

Marmaduke held his gaze for a few seconds, and Jackson wasn't sure what he was going to do. Then he twisted back round, opened the door, and bounced out, sticking the Beretta in his belt under his loose shirt. He moved quickly for a big man. Jackson closed the lock-knife and met him at the back of the car. Marmaduke opened the boot, revealing a silver Colt Python .357 revolver with a two and a half inch barrel, half a dozen small boxes of bullets, and a bag each of white and brown powder. 'You want white, brown, spliff? Man get you anaht'ing.'

Jackson took out his wallet and handed over twelve notes adorned by Errol Barrow. He took the revolver and two of the boxes, 'I'll take the hydrashock and the hollow point bonded. You can take me back to the Sea Breeze now.'

Marmaduke sucked his teeth again, 'You can walk back. Teach you to diss man, tourist motherfucker like you.' He turned and walked off to buy lunch.

Jackson stuffed the revolver into his belt — three-five-seven's weren't designed to be easy to conceal — pocketed the bullets, and walked back to the main road. He hadn't ever killed anyone just because they'd annoyed him.

Yet.

13

Sam Lord's Castle

Jackson and Mary had a light lunch at the Beach Bar, during which he told her they were booked on a helicopter tour at fifteen-thirty. The tour consisted of a forty-five minute flight around the entire coast of the island. Mary's suspicions were confirmed as to the real purpose of the journey when they flew over the huge estate of Sam Lord's Castle, a luxury hotel on the windswept Atlantic Coast in St Philip. Jackson, who had taken the window seat, took as many photos as he could with the digital camera until they left the resort for Hackleton's Cliff.

After dinner in the main restaurant at the Sea Breeze, Jackson had a look at his photos. He asked Mary if she would accompany him to St Philip the next day and take some photos of the immediate area surrounding the hotel. She agreed. Jackson didn't want to risk Raymond seeing him there, but he would do his own reconnaissance further up and down the beach.

While Mary read a magazine on the balcony, Jackson got to work on cleaning the three-five-seven. It looked in good condition, but it was rusty. It was all the salt in the air. He'd gathered various bits and pieces together for a makeshift cleaning kit, but it was hard work without the correct tools. At eleven o'clock Mary wanted to go to bed so Jackson took the revolver out to the balcony. It took him until midnight before he was satisfied it was clean, by which time Mary was sleeping soundly.

Jackson loaded the three-five-seven with six hydrashock shells. They looked new, but you could never tell. He didn't really need the other eighteen rounds. If one of the hydrashock bullets hit Raymond it would flatten to twice its size or more, and the pointed inner tip would drag the metal-jacketed projectile through the man's body. If it hit a bone or major muscle group it would probably lodge, causing massive trauma. If it didn't it would pass through whatever part of the body it had hit and leave a huge exit wound . . . causing massive trauma.

That was the theory, anyway.

Jackson had checked first thing on arrival: Raymond was booked into Sam Lord's Castle until next Saturday. He had arrived with another man and they had adjacent rooms. A bodyguard, no doubt. That gave Jackson five full days to get him alone and kill him.

It should be plenty of time.

★   ★   ★

Moon fumbled for the lamp and looked at his watch: fucking three-thirty. He picked up his mobile phone, 'What!'

'Davy, it's me. Sorry to ring so early, but I thought you might wanna be the first to know.'

'What?'

'It's Raymond.'

'What?'

'The traitor, it's Raymond.'

'How did you find out?'

'One o' me grasses.'

'You're positive?'

'Pukka. Do you want me to phone Hassoun, or are you gonna do it?'

'I'll do it. Cheers, John.'

'No problem, guv, catch you at the office.'

★ ★ ★

'What is it, guv?' Sommer walked into Moon's office.

'Close the door,' said Moon. Sommer did so and then sat. 'Raymond and Hassoun are no longer our problem.'

'How's that?'

'Hassoun's found Raymond.'

'Wot, back in South Africa?'

'No, he's on holiday in Barbados.'

'They gonna lift him there?'

'Hassoun's got the CIA swarming all over the island. He flew out of Alconbury on a military aircraft to direct field operations just a few minutes ago.'

'That'll be the last we see of him, yeah?'

137

'I hope so. There's one more thing.'

'Wot?'

'Our friend Major Wilké is also in Barbados. Customs and Immigration reported his entry at Grantley Adams International Airport on Saturday.'

'Wot the fuck is Jackson up to?'

'Going after Raymond himself?'

'Nah, there's no point.'

'It'll tell you something else, then, John: Hassoun wasn't best pleased when he told me. This time, whether Jackson interferes or not, I reckon he's gonna take him out.'

'He's still pissed off about Oosthuizen?'

'He's got the red mist over something. Either Oosthuizen or something else he's not telling us. Either way, I wouldn't want to be in Jackson's shoes right now.'

'Nah, not running around on your tod in the CIA's backyard.'

★   ★   ★

Jackson was standing on an old stone pier in Long Bay, just north of Sam Lord's Castle. It was just after midnight and the

138

moon cast a spectral light on sea and shore. He looked out into the Atlantic. Somewhere under the water were the reefs on which Samuel Lord Hall was alleged to have made his fortune. It was said he was a pirate who lost his taste for travel, something of a drawback in that line of work. To compensate, he'd hung lanterns in coconut trees to indicate to ships that it was safe to land. When they ran aground on the treacherous reefs in Long Bay, he and his men rowed out and robbed them. Sam Lord the lazy pirate, Jackson mused. If it was true, it was obviously profitable because it had paid for the building of the castle in 1820 and kept Lord in luxury until he died twenty-four years later. Beyond the reef was the Atlantic.

Just the Atlantic.

The nearest land east of here was the tiny island of Fogo, part of the Cape Verde island chain, over one and a half thousand miles away. Beyond that by about another three hundred and fifty was Dakar, Senegal, and Africa. Jackson was a long way from either South Africa or England. And he was standing in what felt like the middle of the ocean, all alone.

He had spent a lot of time worrying about how he was going to get to Raymond without either involving Mary, or being caught or killed himself. Mary had already done more than most would have. She was a good friend, and if things did go wrong for him, he didn't want her affected in any way. And that had been the problem. He'd had no one to ask and he knew his own limitations, knew that he wasn't the cleverest planner for this sort of thing. But then, as these things sometimes did when he was lucky, it had suddenly dawned on Jackson: Raymond thought Oosthuizen was alive.

He had to.

Once he got that idea it was easy to work backwards. Raymond was still enjoying his two week holiday on Barbados. Jackson had killed Oosthuizen last Monday. Raymond had flown out to Barbados on the Sunday before. Jackson had killed Lombard on the Thursday.

So, after Jackson had killed Lombard,

Raymond had probably ordered an officer or agent to protect Dirlewanger. As soon as the SASS had received the information that Jackson was the killer, Raymond had given Oosthuizen the job of eliminating him. Oosthuizen had reported that he, Jackson, and Dirlewanger were all in Aberdeen and that everything was under control. Raymond had flown out to Barbados.

But everything wasn't under control, because Jackson had killed Oosthuizen.

Raymond obviously didn't know that. If he had, he would have flown straight to Britain to take charge of protecting Dirlewanger and the third sleeper. It seemed a strange time to choose to go on holiday, just after a sleeper had been killed, but then perhaps it was ideal because it took him out of the frame for involvement. Raymond was playing a dangerous game, not only selling out the West, but allying himself to the most ruthless terrorist organisation the world had ever known. Mind you, thought Jackson, looking back at the lights of the Sam Lord estate, he was probably being well paid. Very well paid.

Once Jackson had worked out that Raymond wasn't in the know about Dirlewanger and Oosthuizen, it had been simple. All Jackson had done was ring him up, exaggerate his South African accent, and pretend he was Oosthuizen. He was Oosthuizen and Oosthuizen needed to see Raymond urgently. Midnight, the stone pier, no problem. Raymond hadn't been happy to hear Oosthuizen, but then he shouldn't be. If Oosthuizen had turned up on Barbados it was obviously because something had gone wrong in Scotland.

Which left Jackson standing on the stone pier waiting for Raymond to arrive.

Jackson had been on the pier for twenty minutes when he heard the faint sounds of movement below him, sand being compressed and shifted by shoes. He turned to face the steps. He had Gary's forty-five in his right hand hanging loose by his side. The three-five-seven was tucked into his belt. Once the forty-five had arrived he'd decided the three-five-seven would be his back-up, just in case there were problems with it. At least he knew the forty-five worked. Jackson heard a murmuring of hushed voices: Raymond wasn't alone.

He hadn't thought he'd be that lucky.

14

A Murder of One

A dark head, then a body, then a second dark head, came into view as the two men ascended the stairs. Jackson saw Raymond at the same time the man saw him. Raymond stopped about ten metres from him, his companion standing a little to his rear and left, casual and loose.

If there was one man in the SASS that Jackson had hoped Raymond wouldn't have with him, it was that short, slim man with skin the colour of chocolate. Aubrey Mthetwa, like Jackson, was an ex-policeman. Mthetwa had been recruited by the SASS from the South African Police Service Special Task Force, the elite police Special Forces unit. Not only had Mthetwa been an inspector in the STF, he'd also been their youngest weapons instructor before he was approached by the SASS.

Mthetwa was a Zulu and he'd always reminded Jackson of Eddie Murphy in *Beverley Hills Cop*. Except that he was leaner, meaner, and faster.

Jackson knew that Mthetwa would be armed. It would be a small, semiautomatic pistol. Mthetwa always favoured a lighter weapon. He didn't need big, heavy bullets because he was a crack shot with both pistol and rifle. He used eliminators, the very high velocity round with the red plastic tip which he believed was more effective than hydrashock. Jackson also knew there was no way he could beat Mthetwa.

Not now, not ever.

Raymond was a big man with coffee-coloured skin that had a slight yellow tint which always made him look unhealthy. He put his hands on his hips.

Jackson raised the forty-five, 'Hold it.'

Before Jackson could complete the move of raising his arm from waist to shoulder, Mthetwa had moved out to the right, drawn a pistol from somewhere, and adopted the weaver stance, minimising the potential target for Jackson.

Raymond smiled.

'Hello, Aubrey,' said Jackson, 'slowing down a little?'

'What are you doing here, Jackson?' said Raymond.

Jackson lowered the forty-five, 'I've come for you.'

'Why, what business is it of yours?'

'You sold Operation Condor to al-Qaeda.'

Raymond shrugged, 'And you're retired, so it's no concern of yours.'

'Terrorism concerns everyone.'

'Very noble, Jackson, but you always struck me as a bit of an idealist, even if you were a good killer. That was why we had to let you go, you know?'

'I killed whoever you sent me to kill.'

'You did, but we were worried after Canada. I never thought we should use a cop as an assassin, especially not on that job. Actually, I don't like having cops as agents at all. Too much bloody trouble.'

'What about Aubrey?' Jackson nodded his head towards Mthetwa.

'Aubrey is a bodyguard, not an assassin.'

'So you tried to kill me in Italy?'

Raymond shrugged again, 'The order came from Breyten himself, but we all supported it. Not only was it the clever thing to do, it was politically correct as well. But you escaped and ran away to live in England. Hey, who gives a shit? You still haven't told me why you're here.'

'My brother-in-law was killed in Iraq last year.'

'*Ja? Al-Qaeda*'s got *boggeral* to do with Iraq, man, you sound like Bush. How's killing me going to help?'

It was Jackson's turn to smile, 'As Deputy Director General I'd expect you to be better informed, Konnie. You obviously don't know who he was.'

'Why should I?'

'Because he was Colonel Brukman, United States Marine Corps, and I'm holding his service pistol in my hand.'

'Oh.' Raymond stared at Jackson.

Aubrey was like a statue in the gentle onshore breeze. A taught bowstring. His small 7.65mm Beretta was pointed directly at the centre of Jackson's forehead.

'How many SASS personnel know about Condor?'

'Why, are you going to kill them all?' Raymond smiled.

'Not my job. I'm just interested to see how deep the rot has set in.'

'Seeing as you're only one word away from instant death I can tell you that I have about a dozen assistant directors and intelligence officers loyal to me. They don't know the details of Operation Condor, only that by offering me their loyalty they stand to become wealthy. Influential and wealthy. Barry was one, Aubrey's another. And now Aubrey knows it's *al-Qaeda* that we're working with, thanks to your big mouth. But others have probably guessed already, anyway.'

'What about the rest that trained with the Stasi?'

'Don't be so fucking stupid, man. Paul — that's Brigadier Berger — and I had a . . . special bond . . . you might say. He was a closet homosexual, not a good thing to be at that time and place. I met him when I was in Rostock in eighty-three and

I made myself available to him, to his desires. It paid off because he arranged for my return in eighty-eight.'

'He brought me back just to involve me in Condor. There were only five people who knew about it, but none of the others knew I was one of them. Paul was a clever *ou*, you see, he knew their days were numbered; not like the rest of them. Eighty-eight was the only time I ever visited *Normannenstrasse*, you know? They all thought they were going to last forever, just like Hitler, but Paul knew better. And Condor was too good not to use . . . so he gave it to me, to use if and when the Wall fell. And it did.'

Jackson nodded. 'Why *al-Qaeda*?'

'What do you mean?'

'Why did you sell the operation out to *al-Qaeda*?'

'I waited, you see. You don't get given something as good as Condor and just sell it to the first potential buyer out there. No, you wait, you hang on to it. We're not talking a few quick bucks here, we're talking about power beyond your imagination. So I held on for fourteen years. Before I could move I needed to make sure I was safe. The only way I could do that was by making sure the other four men were dead. Paul killed himself in 1991 and I took the opportunity of bumping off Schellong in 1998. Mielke was too risky, but he was very old so I knew I wouldn't have long to wait. Fucking *Boer*. Once he was gone it took me the rest of the year to get rid of Kaminski and then I was ready.

'After September 11, I saw where the future was. I've had Moslem contacts since my Pan-Africanist Security Service days, of course, and I watched the events of the late nineties in South Africa with interest, but didn't get involved. After September 11 I made use of some of my old colleagues to approach *al-Qaeda*. Of course, they couldn't turn it down. And I made sure that I didn't just sell Condor, I sold my services — and those of my group — as well. We're all in this for the long haul and we're going to be on the winning side this time. The West is too obsessed with fair play and decadence to hold out against Moslem fundamentalism much longer. The *Third* World is the future, Jackson.'

'And when you're group finds out they've been working for *al-Qaeda*?'

'What? Aubrey's still got the gun on you, hasn't he? It's a matter of putting your money and your power where your mouth is, so to speak.'

Jackson looked at Mthetwa: he hadn't even flinched.

The corner of Raymond's mouth curled, and then he smiled, 'You know what we've got here, don't you? It's a Mexican stand-off. I always wondered why it's called that and I must admit I'm still at a loss. The only difference here is that I'm not worried, because we both know that the instant that gat moves Aubrey will put a bullet between your eyes. So why don't you put it down, now-now?'

'And you'll let me walk away? You won't, but you're right, I may as well put this away.' It was Jackson's turn to smile. He turned his right hand palm upwards very slowly, adjusted his grip on the forty-five, and eased the hammer down.

He lifted his shirt with his left hand and slowly, using just two fingers, pulled out the three-five-seven revolver. He turned slightly to his left and flung it out to sea. Then he turned back towards Raymond and — still slowly — put the forty-five where the revolver had been.

Aubrey had moved a fraction, just enough to keep the Beretta fixed on Jackson's forehead as he turned.

Raymond relaxed, 'Sweet. Now before Aubrey blows what brains you have into the sea, you'd better tell me what's potting with Barry and you.'

'Aubrey's not going to shoot me; that's why I put my gun away.'

'He'll do what I tell him.'

'He's not going to follow anyone's orders tonight; he's going to look after himself.'

'Tell me about Barry.'

'Aubrey,' Jackson ignored Raymond, 'how do you think I found out about Operation Condor? I'm retired. The CIA came to visit me in England, that's how. You've just heard Konnie admit he's working for *al-Qaeda*, working against

America. The CIA are going to bury him. Him and everyone who is with him . . . '

'Shut the fuck up!' Raymond commanded.

' . . . I'm telling you this because we've worked together and I don't want to see you go down with him. *Ja*, you can run back to South Africa but you've got to get out of the Caribbean first. We're a long way from Jo'burg, but how far from the nearest CIA office? How far is Bridgetown? What are your chances of getting out of Grantley Adams before they grab you?'

'Shoot him!'

'Are you telling me you're with the CIA now, Jackson?' Aubrey spoke for the first time.

'No, but they're after Raymond and they're after me, and I know that they just found out where I am,' Jackson guessed.

'I said, shoot him!'

'They'll be here soon?'

'Before you can get your ass back to KwaZulu, *mfwet*.'

'Aubrey, shoot this fucking bastard or give me the gat and I'll do it myself!'

153

Raymond turned to Mthetwa.

Jackson noted that Aubrey was right about the eliminator rounds, because the single shot took off three-quarters of the back of Raymond's skull.

Aubrey lowered the Beretta while Raymond twitched and foamed and bled on the stones. He looked at Jackson.

'Throw that in the sea, get your bags, and get back to SA.'

'You weren't lying to me?'

'Sooner or later they'll find me. If you're gone by then, they'll assume I killed Konnie.'

'Jackson, you are a good man. I believe to be in your debt.'

Jackson nodded towards Raymond, 'Let's call it even.'

Mthetwa threw the pistol into the sea and bobbed down the stairs onto the beach. A few seconds later disappeared into the shadows.

Jackson leaned against the stone of the pier and watched Raymond die. When he was certain the traitor had taken his last breath, he dragged him to the end of the pier and heaved him over into the

Atlantic. Then he followed Mthetwa and disappeared amongst the palm trees.

★　★　★

Hassoun was not happy.

He hadn't slept in the last forty-eight hours, not when he'd found out first thing on Monday morning that Raymond was the traitor. Early on Wednesday morning an intelligence source had confirmed that Raymond was in Barbados along with a certain John Wilké, Jackson's SO12 alias. That was twelve hours ago and Hassoun had been straight back to the US on a military plane, changed at JFK, and taken an embassy flight to Barbados. A field agent had filled him in on the drive from Grantley Adams to Bridgetown: Raymond was dead. That fucking no good sonofabitch Jackson had killed him. And now Hassoun was mad, real mad. Madder than he'd ever been before in his life.

Jackson would die.

Not only had he completely fucked-up the sting on the SASS, but he'd killed a potential gateway to *al-Qaeda*. That would have been Hassoun's directorship guaranteed. No one had broken into *al-Qaeda* yet, he would have been the first. And now Raymond was dead and so were Hassoun's hopes of rapid promotion. The man was a clear and present danger to US interests and besides, Hassoun's leg still fucking hurt like hell. The man was gonna pay. He was gonna pay with his life.

Hassoun limped into the offices in Broad Street in Bridgetown and headed straight for the shower, telling the officer to bring him lots of coffee and some breakfast. An hour later, with the airport secure and no new information having come to light, he was on his way to the Bridgetown police headquarters when his mobile rang, 'Hassoun!' he barked.

'It's Ben, I've got bad news.'

Hassoun had had about all the bad news he could handle, 'Spit it out, then!'

'This Wilké guy — Jackson — he's gone.'

'Whaddya mean gone! He canta gone! I thought we had this place sown up, it's a

156

tiny fuckin' island for Chrissakes!'

'Yeah, by the time the local cops got it out to the airport he was gone. Flew out to Dublin, Ireland, nine o'clock this AM.'

'Direct, don't tell me it was direct!'

'No, it stopped off in Miami.'

'We'll grab him there! If the plane's still on the goddamn ground we'll grab the sonofabitch there! Do it!'

'The flight left forty-five minutes ago.'

Fuck.

15

Mrs Standfast

Exactly three weeks after Jackson had murdered Lombard with the Russian Dragunov sniper rifle, Moon and Sommer returned to Birch Tree Grove. They waited until quarter-to-nine for Mrs Jackson to leave. When she still hadn't gone, Moon knocked on the door anyway.

Lynley Jackson opened the door. She had her long honey-blonde hair tied tight back in a ponytail and she was wearing a white blouse and fawn slacks. 'I wondered when you were going to knock, you must have been sitting there for half an hour or more. Come inside, you know the way,' her American accent was soft and smooth.

They all sat in the lounge. 'We've come to see your husband, Mrs Jackson, is he here?' asked Moon.

'No, he's visiting my mom in Boston at

present. I'm surprised you didn't know that already, Inspector, I thought that sort of thing was your job. Perhaps I can help you?'

'No, I don't think so. When will he be back?'

'I want you to understand something, and that is not only do I never want to see you again, but I don't ever want you contacting my husband either, unless you have a warrant for his arrest.'

'Yeah, well, talking of that, I think your husband had better head over to my office at New Scotland Yard the moment he gets off his return flight. You can tell him that for me when you speak to him.'

Moon started to rise, but Lynley jumped up, 'You're not listening to me, Inspector. I know all about what's been going on, about Condor, Gary, Hassoun, Aberdeen, everything. You're not leaving here until I'm convinced that you're finished with my husband.'

Moon relaxed back in his seat and Lynley sat down. 'If you want to play it like that, Mrs Jackson, what was your husband doing in Barbados two weeks ago?'

'Jack was never in Barbados, he was in Ireland, visiting a friend. But he knows what happened in Barbados. A man called Raymond was murdered.'

'If your husband was never in Barbados how would he know that?'

'Because he still has friends in the Secret Service.'

'And he was conveniently in Ireland at the time?'

'That's right. He has several witnesses should there be any question. One of them has a daughter who's a police inspector, just like you.'

'And he flew straight from Ireland to Boston?'

'No, he came back here first, last week, then flew from Heathrow a couple days later.'

'If you know all about Condor and everything else, I'm surprised you didn't talk him out of going. You know he's pissed off a high-ranking CIA officer?'

'Yes, and that's exactly why I told him to go and stay with my family. The US is my home and there's no way I'm going to have my husband scared to go back there. Do you understand?'

'Whatever. I'll be very surprised if he makes it back without a little trip to a basement somewhere. In fact it wouldn't surprise me if he never made it back at all.'

'Don't bet on it. I spoke to Erik Hassoun the day Jack left.'

Moon raised his eyebrows, '*You* spoke to Hassoun?'

'I phoned him and I told him that I'd had one of the lawyers from the firm my company uses take a full statement from my husband detailing everything — and I mean everything — that had happened since you were last here. No names have been altered to protect the guilty, Detective Inspector Moon.'

'And I suppose if anything should happen to . . . '

'If my husband and I should die together before we're sixty, the statement, along with a letter and some other things, are being mailed to the *Times*. That's London and New York, by the way. If anything should happen to anyone of us before that and the other thinks it's suspicious . . . I'm sure you understand.'

'You realise that your husband will be exposed as a murderer? You know he shot down an innocent man on his way to work with his wife in the car? There's no statue of limitations on murder.'

'I don't think it will come to that, do you? There are too many people so much more important than my husband who will have their reputations ruined even if they aren't indicted themselves. Don't you think?'

'You're serious?'

'What do you think?'

Moon stood up and Sommer followed suit. 'I think your husband might be in possession of a passport and driver's licence in the name of John Wilké, as well as a US Marine Corps issue Colt .45 service pistol. I want them all,' he held out his hand.

Lynley stood as well. 'Inspector, I'm sure I don't know what you're talking about.'

Moon opened his mouth to say

something, stopped, and lowered his hand.

'Now, do we understand each other?' Lynley continued.

Moon looked at Sommer, who shrugged. 'I don't expect myself or Detective Sergeant Sommer to hear from you or your husband again, either, Mrs Jackson. Have a good life.'

'And a long one,' added Sommer.

Lynley showed them out and closed the door behind them. 'She'd better have a bloody long life, Christ, imagine if they both die in an accident somewhere?'

'I think that's exactly what their insurance covers.'

'The fucking bitch.'

'You know what, guv?' said Sommer as they climbed into the car.

'What?'

'I still think she looks like Elle Macpherson.'

Epilogue

BBC News UK Edition
Last Updated: Thursday, 22 March 2007,
01:43 GMT

North Sea Claims Another Victim

A diving engineer from GlobalSanteFe, the multinational oil company, disappeared from an oil rig in the North Sea. The engineer, identified as Klaus Dirlewanger, is missing presumed dead. He was last seen on Wednesday night by colleagues on the rig. The low temperatures of the North Sea at this time of year make even short term survival unlikely due to hypothermia.

Ms Francis, a spokesperson for the company, expressed their deepest regret for the accident, which they believed could have been caused by the extreme weather which several of the rigs have been experiencing over the last week. Ms

Francis stated that health and safety had always been a priority for Sante Fe, and that their record was one of the best in the industry. Mr Dirlewanger lived in Queens Cross in Aberdeen. He was single and is not believed to be survived by any relatives.

★ ★ ★

BBC News UK Edition
Last Updated: Thursday, 22 March 2007, 13:45 GMT

French Soldier Killed in Shooting Accident

A German volunteer in the French Foreign Legion has been shot dead in an accident at a military training ground outside Marseilles. Joachim Stroop was an adjutant in the 2e Régiment Étranger d'Infantry, based in Nîmes. The report comes amid growing concerns for army training safety standards in France, following the death of a young female recruit in January.

We do hope that you have enjoyed reading this large print book.

Did you know that all of our titles are available for purchase?

We publish a wide range of high quality large print books including:
Romances, Mysteries, Classics
General Fiction
Non Fiction and Westerns

Special interest titles available in large print are:
The Little Oxford Dictionary
Music Book, Song Book
Hymn Book, Service Book

Also available from us courtesy of Oxford University Press:
Young Readers' Dictionary
(large print edition)
Young Readers' Thesaurus
(large print edition)

For further information or a free brochure, please contact us at:
Ulverscroft Large Print Books Ltd.,
The Green, Bradgate Road, Anstey,
Leicester, LE7 7FU, England.
Tel: (00 44) **0116 236 4325**
Fax: (00 44) **0116 234 0205**

Other titles in the
Linford Mystery Library:

DEATH OF A COLLECTOR

John Hall

It's the 1920s. Freddie Darnborough, popular man about town, is invited to a weekend at Devorne Manor. But the host, Sir Jason, is robbed and murdered hours after Freddie's arrival. However, one of the guests is a Detective Chief Inspector. An odd coincidence? The policeman soon arrests a suspicious character lurking in the shrubbery. But Freddie alone believes the man to be innocent. And so, to save an innocent man from the gallows, Freddie himself must find the real murderer.

SHERLOCK HOLMES AND THE GIANT'S HAND

Matthew Book

Three of the great detective's most singular cases, mentioned tantalisingly briefly in the original narratives, are now presented here in full. The curious disappearance of Mr Stanislaus Addleton leads Holmes and Watson ultimately to the mysterious 'Giant's Hand'. What peculiar brand of madness drives Colonel Warburton to repeatedly attack an amiable village vicar? Then there is the murderous tragedy of the Abernetty family, the solving of which hinges on the depth to which the parsley had sunk into the butter on a hot day . . .